ALSO FROM NEW PULP PRESS

Crime Factory: The First Shift, by various authors
badbadbad, by Jesús Ángel García
The Bastard Hand, by Heath Lowrance
The Science of Paul, by Aaron Philip Clark
21 Tales, by Dave Zeltserman
Flight to Darkness, by Gil Brewer
The Red Scarf, by Gil Brewer
A Choice of Nightmares, by Lynn Kostoff
As I Was Cutting, by L.V. Rautenbaumgrabner
Bad Juju, by Jonathan Woods
Rabid Child, by Pete Risley
The Disassembled Man, by Nate Flexer
While The Devil Waits, by Jackson Meeks
Almost Gone, by Stan Richards
The Butcher's Granddaughter, by Michael Lion
In Nine Kinds of Pain, by Leonard Fritz

UPCOMING

A Death in Mexico, by Jonathan Woods

Hell on Church Street

Hell on Church Street

Jake Hinkson

A NEW PULP PRESS BOOK
First Printing, January 2012

Copyright © 2012 by Jake Hinkson

All rights reserved. No part of this book may be reproduced or transmitted in any form or by any electronic or mechanical means including photocopying, recording or by any information storage and retrieval system, without the written permission of the publisher, except where permitted by law.

This book is a work of fiction. Names, characters, places, and incidents either are the products of the author's imagination or are used fictitiously, and any resemblance to actual events or persons, living or dead, is entirely coincidental.

ISBN-13: 978-0-9828436-7-3
ISBN-10: 0-9828436-7-4

Printed in the United States of America

Visit us on the web at www.newpulppress.com

To
JR and Amy,
For giving me a place to sleep

God made everything out of nothing
but the nothingness shows through.

—Paul Valery

Part One:
Bad Men and Termites

Chapter One

I'd been working three weeks at a plastics factory down in Mississippi when the foreman—a bucktoothed redneck named Cyrus Broadway—made the mistake of calling me a lazy asshole. Now, I might be lazy, but I'm also one mean son of a bitch. I've spent time in jails and drunk tanks all over this country, everywhere from a dusty cell at the edge of the Mojave desert to a damp, padlocked shack on an island off the coast of Maine. And nobody gets away with insulting me, even if he thinks he's just kidding. By the time they pulled me off Cyrus Broadway, I'd smashed his face to sausage. His big horse teeth were laying next to him on the factory floor.

I didn't wait around to talk to those Mississippi cops. I left that night and snaked my way up through Louisiana, into Texas and wound up lurking around a Texaco just outside of Sallisaw, Oklahoma. I tried to keep a low profile, but after a couple of days of not eating, I started looking for somebody to stick up. I scoped out a couple of women, but sticking up women is usually more trouble than it's worth. Cops respond faster when there's a woman involved, and if things go bad and you have to rough up a woman—hell, cops love tracking down a woman-beater and kicking the shit out of him. Makes them feel like they're good guys.

So I waited. I let the women go. The teenagers. The

couples. The old man with a van full of dogs. I waited, but I was getting impatient.

When I spotted the fat guy, I knew I'd found my mark.

It wasn't just that he was fat. He was eating his way, and quick, into being too fat for regular clothes. Fat swelled off every part of him and stretched his white dress shirt like a balloon. His hair had faded yellow stains at the tips like he'd dyed it blond at some point.

But there was something else about him, something else that marked him as a loser. It was how he moved. He carried himself like he'd already had the shit beat out of him that night, like every step he took was a battle he was barely winning against gravity.

He parked his beat-up station wagon at the end of the row. As I watched from the shadows, he climbed out, opened the back door and dug his wallet out of the coat hanging off the seat. Without locking the car, he stumbled inside. I watched through the window. Behind me, the interstate was dark and quiet. Occasionally a car passed in the distance and then disappeared back into the black silence. At the counter, my big, fat, easy mark checked his watch and rubbed his eyes. He bought a pack of caffeine pills, three packs of cigarettes, and 24 ounces of Dr. Pepper. He pointed at some chicken wings under the heat lamp, and the cashier piled a heap of them into a box.

As the fat guy came out, dragging himself back to his car, the cashier settled down onto his mop bucket behind the counter so he could watch television. I was pretty sure he couldn't see a thing over the counter. I pulled the gun from my jeans. For the moment, there were no cars at the pumps. When the fat man got his car door open, I stepped from the shadows, slipped up behind him and shoved the gun into the saddlebag of cellulite drooping over his belt.

"Stay calm," I told him, "and get in the car."

He didn't move. Behind us, the interstate didn't make a sound.

I jabbed him with the gun. "Get in the fucking car."

He clutched the door with one hand and rested his other hand on the roof of the station wagon. In a high-pitched voice he said, "Why don't you just take my money and car now?"

I pistol-whipped him—hard, but not too hard, making sure to get some of his ear into it. He slumped into the door and the hinges groaned and the whole damn car tilted. He didn't make a sound, though.

I jammed the gun barrel against his skull. "Get in the fucking car."

Cupping his bloody ear, he climbed in, and I got in behind him. The car reeked of cigarettes and coffee. He started it up and backed out, still holding his ear, not moaning or crying, just holding it like he might be listening to a seashell.

We pulled away from the station and everything was dark inside the car except the green glow of his dashboard. When he pulled to the edge of the parking lot, I said, "Go left" and he did. I had in mind a little field about a mile away where the lights from a cord factory shined down off a hill. It was impossible for anybody up there to really see what you were doing in the field, and if there weren't any drunk teenagers down there, you'd be all alone.

We were about to pass the turn-off to the interstate and I told him, "Keep going straight."

As soon as I said it, he swung the car onto the turn-off and floored the gas.

"Straight, goddamn it," I yelled, but he just picked up speed. I went to hit him again, but he leaned forward, as far as his blubber would allow. The thick roll of fat on his neck pinched out between his block-shaped head and round shoulders. He was so crammed against the wheel he could barely steer, and we ripped through grass and gravel and shot onto the interstate beside a diesel. I flung myself forward on the seat and wedged the gun barrel behind his right ear.

Over the diesel blaring its horn at us I yelled, "I'm going to blow your goddamn head off!"

"And then what?" he asked. The wagon looked like a piece of shit, but it had some get up and go. We were already doing ninety and the diesel's headlights shrunk behind us.

I pressed the gun to his shoulder. "You don't have to die right away," I said. "Slow down."

"Happy to," he said. He slowed down a little, but we were still cruising along.

"Jesus," I said. I wiped some sweat off my lip and rolled down the window. "Stop the car."

"No," he said.

"What?"

"No, I'm not stopping the car."

I shoved the gun against his head, really digging the barrel into the soft part just behind his earlobe.

"This again?" he asked, pressing down on the pedal.

I almost laughed at that. Resting my gun against his seat, I said, "Okay then. What the hell do you want to do now?"

He took a deep breath. "Give me a second," he said. "All this excitement's hard for a fat man." He took another breath, let it out through his nose and pointed the rear-view mirror at me. His eyes were puffy and bloodshot. "You wanted to rob me," he said.

The pale green dashboard lights glowed on his face. He looked damn near dead.

"Yeah," I said.

"That's not going to happen."

I leaned forward and tapped the back of his head with the gun. "That's up for debate."

"I'm not going to let you rob me," he said calmly, "but I'm willing to give you some money. A pretty good amount of money, actually."

"What are talking you about?"

He nodded and settled back into his seat, his head bumping the gun as if it didn't mean anything. I dropped the gun to my knee, but I kept a finger on the trigger. He peeled the cellophane off his cigarettes and pulled one out. He gestured to me. I shook my head. When he lit up, the car filled with smoke. It smelled pretty good.

"On second thought," I said, "give me one."

He pulled out a cigarette and handed it back. I lit it with my own lighter.

He said, "Let's look at your predicament: I'm driving. I've made it clear I'm not just going to just pull over and let you stick me up."

"I still have the gun here," I reminded him.

"Of course," he said. "And I'm still driving. That makes us about even, I'd say."

"Except that I'll probably survive a crash," I said. "And you won't survive a bullet through the back of your brain."

"Good point," he said. His voice was high and girlish, but firm. "Hold that thought. We'll come back to it in a minute. Right now we're at an impasse. You want to rob me. I won't pull over. If I run us into a tree or off an overpass, maybe you'll survive, maybe you won't. Maybe you'll just lose an arm or a leg. But what if we change things up?"

"What do you mean?"

"What if we make a deal, changing this from a robbery gone bad into a business proposition?"

I flicked ashes on his backseat. "I'm listening."

"What you need to understand is that I'm not above giving you money. I can give you three thousand dollars right now. But I want something in return."

Neither of us had opened a window to let the smoke out, and the car was like a rolling gas chamber.

"And what do I have to do for this money?" I asked.

I turned around for some reason to see if we were being followed. Everything was fucked up. We weren't being followed, but I was starting to get worried.

"Where are we going?" I said.

"Driving," he said. "Just driving."

I stared at the back of his head and thought about it. Something was wrong with him, but, on the other hand, I really didn't have a dime in my pockets. I couldn't make him stop the car without wrecking it, and if he did wreck it I might be fucked up and hurt out in the middle of nowhere. I couldn't really do much except wait and see what happened. At least we were moving away from Oklahoma.

"What's your name?" I asked.

"Geoffrey Webb," he answered. "What's yours?"

"What do I have to do for this money, Geoffrey?"

"Nothing. Just ride along with me for a while," he said. He checked his speed. "Yes. I'd say just three or four hours at the outside."

"Just ride around with you?"

"Just sit back there. I haven't talked to anyone in a very long time."

I stared at him. "And?"

He shrugged his big shoulders and took a short drag off his cigarette.

"What are you not telling me?"

"Look," he said, "I—what's your name?"

"Right," I said. "I'm going to tell you my name."

"I find it hard to talk to someone if I don't know his name."

"I guess you'll have to find it hard," I said.

He smiled in the rearview mirror.

"Okay," he said.

"You sick or something?"

He shrugged. "Not physically."

"This sounds a lot like bullshit to me, Geoffrey," I said. "This sounds like you're taking me into some damn trap or something."

He nodded, cracked his window and flipped his butt out. "That's not the case, but I guess I can understand your paranoia. You're a bad man; I get it. You don't know me from Adam, and here I am offering you money to ride with me for a while. You think about it for a minute, though, I'm sure you'll see how absurd the idea of a 'trap' is."

"Where are you going?"

He pulled a greasy napkin from a wadded-up fast food sack and dabbed blood from his ear. "Arkansas."

I didn't say anything.

"Ever been there?" he asked.

"Couple of times."

"What'd you think?"

"Nothing there but weather and sweat."

He smiled. "Well, I'm sure you can make do," he said. He dug out his wallet and tossed it over his shoulder. "It's a simple proposition," he said. "The three thousand is in there."

I opened the wallet. It was fat with hundred-dollar bills. I didn't count it, but it looked to be about right. I looked back up at him. My hands were sweaty for some reason. I knew I could beat the shit out of Geoffrey Webb. I'd already smacked the hell out of him, but he had taken it like it was more inconvenient than anything else. He wasn't afraid of me and he wasn't afraid of the gun, either.

"Okay," I said. I slipped the gun in my coat pocket. "Just drive and shut up for a minute. You make me jumpy blathering on."

He didn't reply to that at all, and we rode for a while in silence. Oklahoma rolled past like a flat black nothing.

I watched him in the rearview mirror. He glanced at me and then back at the road.

"What's your deal?" I said.

"What do you mean?"

"You know what I mean."

He smiled. "You wanted me to stay quiet, I thought."

"I changed my mind."

"Good," he said. "I haven't had a real conversation in years."

"Hard to believe, talky fucker like you."

"I've always been a good talker. Talked my way out of a lot of trouble. A lot of trouble."

I could believe it. I'd known plenty of con men, guys who could talk the stink off of shit. And Webb talked like a con man who'd been out of business for a long time but still had some juice inside him.

"Then what's the problem?" I said.

"There's a level of trouble you can't talk your way out of," he said. "Some trouble is like a cancer. It just grows inside you. Nothing stops it. It just keeps growing and growing, eating everything it touches."

"Then what?"

"You die." He took a deep breath and lit up another cigarette. "But I've been living like I was dead for years now. I've been a walking shadow, like Shakespeare wrote about."

"Shakespeare."

He looked at me in the rearview mirror.

"Yeah, I've read a few books," he said. "I used to read a lot. I used to do a lot of things."

"So what happened?"

"The story of my life?"

"Whatever."

He shrugged. "The story of my life is I lived, I fucked up, and I'm going to die. I'll probably go to hell."

I stubbed out my butt on his car seat. He didn't seem to notice. He was too busy listening to himself talk.

"That's cheery, I know," he said, "but it's the truth. I've been living like a termite for years now: smoking, eating shit, working the nightshift at a supermarket. No kind of life. No friends. No family. The only emotion I ever feel anymore, when I feel anything at all, is fear."

"Fear of what? You obviously ain't afraid to die."

"No. But you can get to a point where you're more afraid of living than dying."

He sat there silent for awhile. I didn't have anything to say to that. Life sucked, sure, but what else was there? Nothing?

"Living like a termite is my punishment," he said.

"For what?"

"Sins."

"Which ones?"

"You want to know?"

"Ain't got anything else to do until we hit Arkansas."

"I'll tell you," he said. "I've never told anyone, but I'll tell you. You look at me and you see a fat slob, a sucker, a potential victim. Right?"

I just stared at him.

"Fine," he said, "I'm not an intimidating man. Believe me, I know. But I'm not talking about being intimidating. I used to be the safest man you could imagine. At one time, years ago, so many people loved me and trusted me you wouldn't believe it. I've known the kind of trust that few people are ever afforded. And I betrayed it. So now I guess I deserve the termite life I've been living. I deserve to die the way I'm going to die. I betrayed everyone who ever trusted me, and God saw fit to cast me down with the termites. No amount of forgiveness or understanding will change what I've done."

He glanced back at me.

I told him, "Pass me those cigarettes."

As he passed a pack back to me, he smiled the oddest smile. "I'll tell you why I'm going to hell," he said. "You'll soon agree I deserve it."

Part Two:
Hell on Church Street

Chapter Two

To begin at the beginning: I had an abusive father—I know, my kind always does, but we're a regenerating lot of bastards. Sin begets sin. My father was a mean drunk, as was his father before him, and on and on, back, probably, to Lot, that original disgusting drunk in the Bible who, while on the booze, banged his two daughters. Not just one daughter, mind you, but both, and apparently at the same time. If drunken group sex with your own daughters doesn't qualify you for the termite colony, nothing will.

Anyway, my father was a sadistic fuck who worked as a RN at a little hospital on the outskirts of Little Rock. He was smart, you see, but he was sick. He would sit on our back porch after work drinking beer and shooting at the trees with his .22.

Once, when I was about eleven, he told me to go pick up a branch he'd blasted off a pine tree with repeated shooting, and as I walked out to the branch, he lifted the gun to his shoulder. I looked back and saw him and he was smiling, a thin twisted little smile that made him look like the Joker. I started to shake. "Pick up that branch," he called without moving the gun. The sight on the barrel obscured his eye, and I began to cry. "Pick up that fucking branch," he yelled. "You pick up that branch right now, you pussy." I crumbled to the ground, and he fired the gun. I wet myself and realized then that he'd fired the gun in the air. He didn't say anything more about the branch.

So you see, it's all my father's fault.

As for my mother, what can I say about her except that she was the type of woman who would marry my father. They divorced when I was thirteen. I stayed with her, of course, which thrilled her not one little bit, but she did enjoy suing him for child support. He kept threatening to kill her, which I think secretly turned her on, and he was sent to jail for a time. Not long after he went away, Mom left me with her mother-in-law and ran off. The last time I tried to track her down, I found that she'd been working as a prostitute around truck stops in Texarkana.

It was my uncle Ronald—my mother's little brother and a surprisingly sane human being—who first took me to church when I was fifteen. He was dull and balding, with a fat wife and a crappy job at Maytag, but he was a nice man who thought church might do me some good.

And it did.

It's difficult to say now if I would have been any worse without the church, as the church played such a pivotal part in the undoing of my life. I don't know. I do know that as a rawboned teenager I had nowhere else to go. At school I was an anathema to most people. I was nerdy, but lazy about homework, so I wasn't considered smart. I always said the wrong thing at the wrong time, so I wasn't considered quick or funny. To make matters worse, I'd inherited my father's lanky body and my mother's dull face and looked, I thought, like a very homely girl. I was really small in those days. Becoming fat has been an act of the utmost will. Back then I was a geek, everyone's geek. I was the geek even the geeks could look down on, the salve to everyone's shaky self-esteem.

The Baptist Church, and in particular the youth group, changed that. What I discovered at the youth group was *not* that I was suddenly popular, or even that I suddenly had friends. No, what I discovered was that they had to accept me. They were obligated to accept me. My youth minister was a former outcast like myself, a portly, red faced young guy named Leonard. He reached out to me, as they say, and told me God loved me.

Now, of course, I didn't believe that. Nothing in my fifteen years would have served as proof of God's existence, much less as proof of his love. I was underwhelmed by the fact that Jesus Christ of Nazareth had been executed by the Roman Empire two thousand years before my birth. One might as well say I should feel God's love because John Wilkes Booth shot Abe Lincoln in the back of the head. Scripture said that we should consider the sparrow and God's care of it, but I'd seen birds lying dead on the side of the road, their corpses being picked apart by ants. So I knew it wasn't true that God loved me, but I said I believed it and I was baptized because what I *did* believe was that the people at the church felt they had that obligation to me. If it was some idea of God's love that made them duty-bound to accept me, so be it.

Our church was a modest country congregation with only a few hundred people attending on a regular basis. The youth group numbered about thirty, and I soon found that I was able to rise among these ranks into someone who was genuinely accepted and even, on some occasions, liked. I even found, much to my delight, that my Christian friends were forced to acknowledge me as a peer at school. After fifteen years, I'd found my niche.

I'd also found a profession. Brother Leonard became my hero, and as I watched him work over the next few years I began to realize that his job was a sick joke.

I mean, the ministry *can* be a hard job. Ministers see people at their worst, and they are sometimes called on to mediate the most contentious of disputes and bear witness to the worst of human tragedies. They are expected to bring light into utter darkness.

But that's exactly why, for the most part, religion's a scam. For all its history and prestige, for all the buildings built to honor it and all the blood spilt to propagate it, religion is no different than reading palms or staring at tea leaves.

Leonard, he of the big heart and wide smile, probably didn't work more than three hours a week. But he got paid like he worked fifty! He was supporting a wife and two teenaged kids *by reading Bible stories on Wednesday night*. This was not lost on me.

It hit me like divine inspiration. Religion is the greatest graft ever invented because no one *ever* loses money claiming to speak for the invisible man in the sky. People already believe in him. They already accept they owe him money, and they think they'll burn in hell if they don't pay him. If you can't make money in the religion business, you need to give up.

Chapter Three

A few months out of college, I got my first job as a youth minister at a place called Higher Living Baptist Church in the southwest section of Little Rock. They were looking for a youth pastor, and Leonard knew the preacher and thought he'd take a chance on a kid fresh out of school.

Leonard had convinced me that I needed to go to a little junior college and pick up a two year degree in communications. The classes themselves were boring, except for the Speech class, which was terrifying. I got through the class okay, though, and learned something valuable about myself: I could speak in front of people. The first time I got up to talk, my voice disappeared. Once I found it, I sounded like a timid bird. But slowly I began to loosen up. I hit my stride in that class when I realized the first fundamental truth of this life: most people just want you to tell them what they want to hear. Double-check me on that; you'll find that it's true. Most folks are happy if you just maintain the balance in their lives.

Once I figured out how to do that—and I was already doing it on a smaller scale, with people like Brother Leonard—I was ready.

I drove down to Little Rock in the snow and met the preacher and let him look me over. He was a dim little guy named Brother Card, a fool, but he didn't know it, and I didn't tell him. There's no bigger fool than the one who thinks he's wise, so from the start, I could tell Brother Card wasn't going to give me any trouble.

The first time I met him, he was sitting at his desk printing off the outline of his sermon. His office was cold because he was trying to cut back on the heating bill. That should tell you what you need to know about the church. It was a rundown place with a small sanctuary, a handful of classrooms, one reception hall where the youth group met on Wednesdays, and the preacher's shabby office. I walked in and knocked on the door. "Brother Card?"

He looked up from his computer. The old printer on the desk next to him rattled and spat out his sermon. "Yes," he said. Despite the cold, his balding head gleamed with sweat.

I told him who I was.

He smiled and stood up. He was taller than me, with no chin and a round gut stretched against a bright red t-shirt that read: *Ask Me About Jesus*. "Good to meet you," he said. I went over to his desk and we shook hands. "You're a protégé of Leonard's, right?" He motioned to the visitor's chair opposite his desk.

We sat down, and I said, "Yes, sir."

"Good fella that Leonard."

"Yes, sir."

"Good man of the Lord."

"Yes, sir, he is."

You see how it went. Card told me I would have to meet the congregation and the youth group, and then the church would vote on me.

"Yes, sir, I understand. I'm really optimistic about being here. The Lord has given me a strong sense he wants me to be here."

Card nodded and shut down his computer. Then he leaned

back. "The youth minister's position is massively important," he said, pressing his fingertips together. "I can't stress that enough."

"Yes, sir."

"The challenges our young people face today are the toughest of any generation in the history of our country."

"Absolutely," I said. "They need guidance more than ever."

"Boy, you said something there. With the television and music and magazines out there…"

"All sex and violence."

He shook his head sadly. "It is. We've got to compete. The church has got to compete against an adversary of incredible power…"

"Yes, sir, it's true."

"While making it clear that our side will win."

"'No weapon formed against us shall prosper,'" I quoted.

"Amen to that," he said with a smile. "I've got a good feeling about you."

I met the rest of the church the following Sunday and the youth group on the following Wednesday. It wasn't too hard. Just told them what they wanted to hear. I preached a little sermon on Wednesday. I gave my best, all around stump speech. A good youth sermon, I'd figured out, has three parts: 1) The world is evil, 2) your parents and the church are good, and 3) you have to choose between 1 and 2.

Now I'm more eloquent than that, or I was, but those were the basic elements. I polished it all off with the story of my tragic childhood and glorious salvation and they nearly cheered me at the end. It's exactly what the people wanted to hear, and it went over like gold with the Higher Living Baptists. They voted me in as youth minister.

Afterwards everyone came up and shook my hand, and that was the first time I met her.

She was sixteen or seventeen years old, and she was nearly invisible. Unattractive and overweight, she drifted among the people of her church touching no one. Unspeaking, she stared at the floor. Her hair, pale blonde to the point of being colorless, draped her shoulders. When she stepped up to shake my hand and lifted her empty blue eyes to my face, her thick mouth jarred itself loose from a perpetual pout into something approaching a nervous smile, and she gave me only the briefest, perfunctory "Hello," but the moment our hands touched an overwhelming desire for her consumed me. How can I explain it? She was not pretty, nor was she evocatively dressed. In fact, her drab green sweatshirt and long denim skirt seemed designed to make her as sensual as sheetrock. Was it that she *was* unattractive, that she was such easy pickings? That night I met other girls, pretty girls, and none of them moved me in the slightest. With her sad face and her bland clothing, this girl simply seemed more real to me. It's safe to say that she seemed more real to me at that moment than anyone else ever had in my life.

Nothing in her face betrayed any desire, any recognition. She let go of my hand and moved on. I watched her go, not wanting to gawk for too long, and I resumed shaking hands with the rest of the congregation.

I was a changed man, though. I was thinking only of *her*. I knew something had happened, something wonderful, but something terrible, too. Loneliness, that vast emptiness, had always extended around me in every direction. I had spent my life as a speck of dirt in an endless world of white. But when I saw *her,* I thought that things might change.

I also knew, however, the danger this brought with it.

I was contemplating this when a portly woman with dyed

black hair walked up to me and announced herself, "Sister Card."

"Sister Card, so nice to meet you," I said, snapping out of my reverie. I was very quick to suck up to all the right people back then. The pastor's wife was someone it would pay to be nice to.

She held onto my hand in that way church people tend to do. I'd noticed Leonard had perfected the hand-gripping conversation.

I held her hand and smiled and nodded while she told me, "We're so glad to have you here. You'll have to come over for dinner some night this week."

"I'd be pleased," I said.

A young, good looking guy slid up next to her and told us, "I'm sorry to interrupt, but I've got to get out of here and I didn't want to go before I met the new man."

Sister Card released her grip on me. My hand felt sweaty and vile, so I wiped it ever so discretely on my leg while she introduced the handsome man. "This is Nick Hargrove, one of our deacons," she said. "Nick's one of our bright young men."

I put that little piece of information into a file in the back of my head. Bright young men are often problems.

Nick just shrugged. He was tall and lanky, with a big nose and thick eyebrows, but somehow he hung together just right, as if through a force of will. "I do what I can," he said. "I just want you to know we're all behind you," he told me. Then he gave me an enthusiastic handshake of the ex-jock variety. "We're looking for you to take these kids to the next level."

I won't disgrace myself by repeating the tired, Vincent Lombardi-meets-Apostle Paul bullshit platitudes I fed him, but he seemed to like it and said goodbye to us.

"A good man," Sister Card told me. "He'll be running this church one day."

Behind Sister Card, *she* walked by again and Sister Card motioned at her. The girl turned and came toward us. My heart slowed and I felt sweat trickle down my scalp. She looked at me and smiled—a polite smile only, but a smile that made me want to fall down. Sister Card said, "You've met our daughter, Angela."

I almost yelped when she said it, but I just nodded. "Yes. I believe we met briefly."

Angela didn't look at me and told her mother, "I'm going outside."

"Okay," Sister Card said. She watched her daughter wander out of the room. Then she patted my back. "It will do her good, I think, to have another positive role model in this church."

"I hope so," I said.

"So how about coming over on Tuesday night? Would that be good for you?"

"It would be divine," I said.

I spent the next day setting up my new home. I'd been given a small, white clapboard house that was less than five minutes away from Brother Card's parsonage and ten minutes away from the church. We were all located on Church Street: me on one end, the Cards in the middle, the church at the other end. My little shack had originally been the home of some ancient pillar of the church who had maintained in her will that the house be set aside for the youth minister or sold to profit the youth group.

Brother Card explained to me the old lady had a "burden for the young people" which is churchspeak for "she liked kids" and he'd never even entertained the idea of selling the house.

So I moved in and didn't have to pay rent. The house was too small for more than one person to live there, and it smelled like mothballs and old linen, but I aired it out, bought some candles and moved in my stuff. Now, since this was pre-internet, I had acquired by that time a substantial pornographic VCR collection. I knew that the discovery of this little treasure trove would be the end of my career, so I had it situated neatly in a locked trunk in my closet. I kept the VCR in the bedroom and the key to the trunk in my pocket.

That night, however, as I sat watching a video of a woman having sex with two men, my thoughts drifted. I thought of Angela—not pornographic thoughts, understand. These were clean thoughts, thoughts of marriage, of babies. I'm not a monster, you know. I dreamed of being married to Angela and being a preacher and having the youth group over to the house to watch Christian videos and eat popcorn. Square fantasies, you understand. Fantasies of normalcy and virtue. As the woman on the screen was turned into a human sponge, I dreamed of holding my sweet Angela's hand and telling her how very much I loved her.

So, you see, starting out I had good intentions.

Chapter Four

When I showed up at the Cards' house for dinner, I was wearing a turtleneck, clean khakis and some new penny loafers. I looked like a geek, but that helped, too. I had gotten a little bigger since school, but I was still a slight man, skinny and pale, and my hair had begun to thin a little. I wore glasses, and I had attempted a beard but nothing much happened there. My chin wouldn't produce more than a few pathetic wires, so I gave up trying to look like a man's idea of a man and opted instead for the small, sensitive look. People seemed to like it, all in all. Women weren't drawn to me, of course, but I looked (and acted) harmless and people tended to regard me that way.

It goes back to that fundamental truth of life I was talking about earlier. People *wanted* me to be a geek. They wanted me harmless and meek. The timidity I wore as a mask was a comfort to people: *well, we know he's okay. Look at him.* Women could assume I was sweet; men could assume I was weak. It's what everyone wanted; I made them all feel good about themselves. And hell, sometimes I felt good about making them feel good.

Sister Card answered the door wearing a t-shirt with a picture of puppies on it. She smelled like onions, and in her left hand she held a butcher knife. I looked down and ever so causally noted the knife.

"I hope that's not for me," I said.

She looked down at the knife and burst into laughter. "No. I completely forgot I was holding it. Heck, that must look odd."

I shook my head, and she let me into the house. It was warm and bright. Thomas Kincaid prints of small country homes hung on the wall. The television was blaring in the living room, but no one was watching it.

She gestured at a long blue sofa. "You can sit down if you'd like. Brother Card will be out in a minute."

I said okay, but I thought it odd that she was relegating me to the living room. I took this as a sign she didn't like me—a suspicion I was rarely wrong about with people.

"Would you like a drink?" she asked as she walked toward the kitchen. "We have Cokes and sweet tea."

"No thank you," I said. I took my seat on the couch, and she retreated into the kitchen. I watched her go. From where I sat, I could see a scented candle burning in the middle of a long dining room table.

I looked around. The coffee table was wrought iron with a freshly cleaned glass top. On the television, some steroid-thickened gorillas chased a football down a snowy field while a freezing congregation of the brainless cheered them. Turning away from that, I noticed pictures of the family along the wall. I stood up and investigated them.

There she was. Angela—or a collection of different Angelas, like variations on a theme: a little girl in blonde pigtails and a Pac-Man shirt holding a paint brush and a turtle with a shiny pink shell; a pimply twelve year-old with a noticeable gut and a barely perceivable training bra, standing with her older brother in front of the house; and finally, a teenager squeezed into a flag line outfit, a smile on her wide face as she poses with a much thinner, prettier cheerleader.

I stared into her eyes. Was there anything there? Anything crying out for help?

"That's the family wall," she said.

I turned and she stood at the entrance to a long hallway. She was wearing a plain blue t-shirt and shorts.

"Yeah," I said calmly. I pointed at the family picture in the middle. "Is this your brother?"

She nodded. "Yeah. Gabe. He's twenty-seven."

"Hmm. Where's he at?"

She seemed bored by the question and flopped down on the stuffed chair next to the couch. "He's in grad school in Illinois." Hands in her lap, knees close together, she stared at the television.

I sat down in the easy chair next to her. My hands were moist and my scalp itched. "Do you like football?" I asked.

Wrinkling her soft brow she said, "Not really, but it's the only television in the house. My father likes to watch it."

Being an astute observer of people, I noted that the term *my father* (as opposed to *Dad*) was a distant one. It was a title, not a name. It didn't have to mean anything, but it was something to tuck away.

"But not you," I said.

"I like basketball," she said and smiled, and something in how she said it told me she was in love with a basketball player.

"Basketball's cool," I said.

"Did you play sports?" she asked.

"No," I said. "I have the physical prowess of a hippopotamus."

She laughed—a sweet, involuntary little giggle. I was pleased she didn't seem to take my sarcasm as a fat joke.

Sister Card came into the room. She was still holding that goddamn butcher knife.

"What's the joke?" she asked with a smile plastered on her face.

Could she see through me?

"Nothing," her daughter said. She didn't sulk when she said it, but the warmth went out of her.

"Well, why don't you help me finish dinner, Angela?" Sister Card said.

The girl shot me a look, and I had to walk a very thin wire in returning it. I couldn't roll my eyes—that would be too much—but I gave her a little grin that could be interpreted by her mother as *See you later, kid. Do what your mother says,* but could also be read by the girl as *I think she's stupid, too.*

It worked, and she grinned back and passed Brother Card on her way out of the room. He and I shook hands.

He wore slacks and a short-sleeve button-up dress shirt and looked like he'd just come from the church. "Sorry to be so long," he said. "I was on the phone with Mrs. Dyess."

I won't bore you with his inane conversation over the next fifteen minutes, but much of it surrounded this Mrs. Dyess, an old widow in the church who was fighting off a terminal case of cancer. I acted interested (no, I acted concerned, *moved* even), quoted scriptures and promised to pray for her. Card, satisfied, finally sat back in the chair and stared at the television.

"Your daughter told me she doesn't like football," I said.

"Did she?" He watched the quarterback lick his fingers.

"Said she was more of a basketball fan."

He turned slowly and looked at me and then glanced back at the kitchen doorway. We could hear running water and the beeping of a microwave. Leaning in he said, "It's this boy at school. He's on the basketball team." He shook his head. "Brother, you don't know what worry is until you have a child, until you have a girl. My boy, Gabe, he's always been fine. Good grades, kept his head about girls, and now he's off in school studying to be a periodontist. I'm sure he's lived it up a little, but he always stayed in church, always stayed close to the Lord." He hung his head. "But Angela…"

"You've had problems?"

He jerked his head toward the kitchen and stood up. I followed him and we walked through the kitchen—where Sister Card was pulling a tinfoil-covered dish from the oven and Angela was sitting at the island twirling salad tongs on her index finger—and Sister Card gave us a five minute deadline for dinner. Angela watched me as I followed her father through a door and into the backyard. The air was bitter, but Brother Card didn't mind. I stuck my hands in my pockets.

"She's never had quite the same head on her shoulders that Gabe has," Brother Card said. He hooked his thumbs on the empty belt loops on his slacks and whistled. "I don't know. You pray for them, you raise them in the ways of the Lord, but at the end of the day they have to decide on their own."

"What is it about this boy on the basketball team that you disapprove of?" I asked.

He took a deep breath. "He's Catholic." Shaking his head, he said, "I talked to her. I sat Angela down in my office at the church, just like I would anyone else, and I said, 'Do you believe that Mary was some sort of goddess?' And she said, 'No.' And I said, 'Do you see anywhere in the Bible where it says we should pray to statues?' And she said, 'No.' 'Well, do you think we should commit ourselves to people who do?' And again, she says, 'No.' So I explained that dating was a big thing and that we shouldn't date the unsaved because the Lord told us not to be unequally yoked together with unbelievers."

"What'd she say?"

He shook his head and kicked a rock. "Oh, she tried to tell

me that Catholics weren't idolaters, weren't drunks, weren't worshippers of that pagan in Rome." Abruptly, he looked at me, so nakedly seeking affirmation that I wanted to laugh in his face. The second fundamental truth of this life is this: we only really trust people who share our prejudices.

"Catholics are the world's biggest cult," I said.

He nodded vigorously. It was freezing, but he didn't seem to notice. "I agree," he said. "And it's not bigoted to say it, is it?"

"Absolutely not. We're supposed to proclaim the truth."

His entire body moved in approval, head nodding, hands rubbing together, feet moving closer to me. "Exactly. I told her that, too. The truth is Jesus and nothing else. No Pope, no priest, no statue of Peter. There's only Jesus and once you pass him by—or once you try to add things to him or take things away from him—then there's a short drop off into nothingness."

I was shivering, but he was oblivious to it. You greedy fuck, I thought. You don't even notice hypothermia overtaking me. Staring at me and talking about your daughter and your desire to protect her from fucking Catholics. Are you crazy? Are you really so stupid?

He kept raving about Catholics, stopping every so often to assure me he didn't hate them, and the entire time I was freezing to death, my fingers and nose starting to burn with coldness.

Finally, my savior opened the door. She leaned out of that warm kitchen and said, "Hey, you two Eskimos. Dinner's ready."

Her father gave her a little smile. "Thanks, sweetie."

She closed the door, and Brother Card's smile turned truly sad for the first time. "Of course," he said, "the worst part is, this boy completely rejects her. Thinks she's fat."

• • •

Dinner was instructive. Sister Card made some kind of meaty casserole and served it with vegetables and garlic bread. Brother Card talked about the local football team and people in the church. I held up my end of the conversation, going on about youth groups and youth rallies and the need for a better national outreach program for the youth—youth, youth, youth. Angela interjected occasionally but mostly she seemed distracted, thinking, I suppose, about her Catholic basketball player.

Sister Card barely spoke and I sensed this was unusual. She didn't openly challenge me on any point, but her entire bearing toward me was distant. She rarely looked at me, and when she did, she stared. "Really?" she would say. Or, "Is that so?" These tiny retorts had the smallest hint of acid in them. When it came time for me to leave, she looked absolutely unburdened. She didn't say anything, of course, but I knew I had flunked some kind of test with her. She was one of those people you could offend and never know how you did it.

"Bye now," was all Angela said before she turned and headed off to her room. I watched her go, her young body full of life and energy. She wasn't beautiful, but she had a quality. She needed to lose weight, fifty or sixty pounds, maybe more, but she was still healthy and young and, in her way, pretty. My body leapt alive when she said, Bye now, turning, her hair slapping her shoulders. I wanted her, wanted to conquer her, wanted that healthy youthfulness for myself and no one else.

She turned and the moment exploded. Her body underneath her clothes, her hair, her voice—Bye now—her complete dismissal of me. I knew she wasn't thinking of me as she turned to leave. She was seventeen, in love with some fool at school, some boy, and I was her geeky youth minister. I worked for her father. I was his friend. But she liked me, and she didn't like him very much right now. She trusted me already and could come to trust me more until one day she trusted me more than anyone else.

She turned (and turned and turned) and I wanted to turn with her, to follow her down the hall, into her room, into her private world, into her soul.

Or is that something I'm just telling you to make myself look better?

My whole life has been a long, tangled series of lies designed to make me look better than I am. Maybe I loved her and wanted to spend forever with her. Maybe I just wanted to follow her into that room and rip off her clothes and throw her on the bed. Maybe her body—imperfect as it was—was all I wanted, after all. I really don't know anymore. These things are a jumble to me now. I can drudge up a mix of truths and lies from the past, but the original distinction between truth and lie has long since disappeared. Worse still are my attempts to remember how I felt. I am sure I felt love. And surely at some time I have operated philanthropically.

But that's not what I *remember*. What I remember is the hunger. Maybe I just wanted that moment on top of her. No matter how good I am at articulating the opposite, maybe that moment is all there is for someone like me.

Chapter Five

I needed a plan. My life thus far had been run without any large plan. It had progressed, stage by stage, in small steps, each designed to secure some small measure of comfort from the harshness and horrors of this world. The ministry was an easy job. I was around nice people—or let's say "nice" people—all the time. I gave them want they wanted, and they took surprisingly little in return. But now I had something *I* wanted.

So I needed a plan. The first thing was to steal Angela away from this kid she was infatuated with. Of course, that would be easy enough because he'd already rejected her. But I already had a lot of experience at watching people, and I suspected that she had that masochistic kind of love for him that compels you to love the more you're rejected. I got my first chance to observe them interacting a few weeks later when he arrived at church one Wednesday night.

We were holding services in the Fellowship Hall at the end of the church's classrooms. The kids milled around talking and drinking colas and munching on potato chips while their parents stood around the snack tables and did the same.

I stood at the podium at the front of a large group of chairs and looked over my notes for the night's lesson. It was the same sermon with a different spin. I was going to talk about why kids shouldn't drink, citing all the biblical warnings against drunkenness and so forth. What I was really doing, and what I was really always doing, was watching Angela. She was standing against the wall with her two friends. One was a fat, black girl with skin the color of chocolate pudding, and the other was fat, white and pimply, with skin like Tapioca pudding. I think Angela kept the pudding sisters around to make herself look better. When the boy strolled in, oblivious to them, they all smiled like fools.

His name was Oscar—a stupid name for an eighteen year old. He was a tall, muscular boy with dark hair flapping over his ears and a tanned complexion that accentuated his caramel-colored eyes. With his confident jock stride and a big, easy smile, it was easy to understand what my love must have seen in him. He was the type that impressionable, insecure girls worship. I'd seen it a thousand times. They love these guys for their assurance, for their ease with the world. It's more hero-worship than love.

He came in with a kid named T.J., a Baptist version of Oscar. The boys drifted over to some popular girls and began talking. Angela watched Oscar as if beams of light were shooting out of his fingertips.

I walked over to him.

"Hi," I said, extending my hand. I told him who I was and said I didn't believe we'd met.

"Oscar," he said, pumping my hand. He had a strong handshake, and I gave it back to him as best I could.

"Great to meet you," I said. There was nothing odd about it. I was just the friendly youth minister. "You came with T.J. here."

"Yeah," T.J. said. He shifted on his feet, and the girls looked at each other. They all seemed to want me to leave.

"They play basketball together," their PR person—a petite

redheaded girl—told me. Leaning against the wall, Angela crossed her arms over her stomach and chewed her bottom lip.

"Do you go to church anywhere?" I asked Oscar.

Again the stupid grin and big alabaster teeth. "Yeah," he said. "Over at St. Mary Magdalene."

I smiled. How nice. "Well, it's great to have you here." I made my exit and retreated to the other side of the room. Angela watched him some more as the pudding sisters whispered in each other's ears and giggled. When it wasn't obvious, I snuck out and went down the hall.

Brother Card was in his office. He stayed in there a lot. I'm not sure what he did. When I was in my office, which wasn't often, I didn't do anything but sleep.

"Howdy," he said. "How goes it?"

"Very well," I said. "Looks like we have a good turnout tonight."

"Good."

I needed to ease into this. "Lot of new kids," I said. "You know, I think the best ministers for the Lord are our youth themselves. No one can reach a kid like another kid."

He propped his elbows up on the desk and rested his chin on his knuckles. "Absolutely. I've always thought that. I think the Lord is using you as a real motivator in that department, too."

And on and on. We always talked like that, Brother Card and I, giving each other imbecilic little lectures on what God was doing, constantly defining and redefining the Good Lord's "actions" and "will." If God exists, then I think he only invented mankind so someone would know he exists. Well, that and he needed a show to watch. If not for the stupid, petty little antics of humanity, what would he be doing with eternity?

Anyway, Brother Card and I rattled on for a few moments before I threw out the hook.

"T.J. brought a kid tonight. Nice kid."

He bit. "Oh yeah?"

"Yeah. Another basketball player, goes to St. Mary's."

The hook set, and Brother Card looked like a fish suddenly realizing that his easy meal is yanking him out of the water.

He just stared at me, and I stared back, faking the dawning of a realization and said, "Is it that boy…"

"Oscar."

"Oscar, right. I think that's his name. Oh well, it's good that he's here, I suppose."

Card leaned back in his chair and chewed on a knuckle. "Yes. Of course. But I wonder…"

It's always funny to watch someone—especially someone as transparent as Brother Card—pulled between what they feel and what they *should* feel. He wanted to run downstairs and kick Oscar's papist-loving ass out the door, but he knew he shouldn't. Maybe Oscar would come to know Jesus—the real, Baptist Jesus. There was always hope and prayer.

But I wasn't about to let hope and prayer get in my way.

"You know I didn't make the connection," I said. "I'm pretty dense sometimes. But now that you mention it, they were together, Angela and Oscar."

"Together?"

"Flirting and laughing. Strictly above board, of course. They seemed to be enjoying a private joke."

"Joke?"

"Like he was here only to see her and they didn't think anyone would notice. I can see it now that you mention it."

He was genuinely perplexed now. "That's what I was afraid of," he said. "But I thought he didn't like her."

"Oh, he likes her," I said. "Still, he seems like a decent boy to me."

"His decency isn't at question here," Card spat back. I looked chastened and ready for enlightenment. He gave it. "What's at question is his susceptibility to the prodding of the Holy Spirit, a susceptibility he's unlikely to have gotten at an altar of the Virgin Mary."

"Very true," I said, shaking my head as if I thought it was the most profound thing ever said and I was disappointed I hadn't thought of it myself. "Very true."

Card said, "You bet it is." Only a man who made his living being meek could have accepted my ass-kissing so causally.

"What should we do?" I asked.

"Nothing for now, of course. I'll talk to her tonight." His face was tight with worry, the worry of a man with an unattractive daughter. All fathers fear that boys are predators, but the father of an unattractive daughter lives in terror of his daughter's own low self-esteem.

I looked at my watch and said I'd better be getting down the hall but, "Maybe it would be best if you don't mention that I was the one who spilled the beans. For the sake of my ministry with your daughter. She might very well hold it against me and I'm afraid that…"

"You're right," he said. "She needs to feel she can come to you about this or anything else."

I nodded. "Exactly. I'm sorry to have been the one to bring this to your attention."

He waved that away. "Glad you did. We'll pray about it, and I'll talk to Angela and her mother."

I said I'd pray about it and left.

Back down the hall the kids were taking their seats. I preached them a good message that night on the dangers of alcohol. I was above reproach when it came to drinking, as I had never done it. Isn't that sad? Never touched the stuff.

I preached it a little harder than usual since I was worked up about my love and her basketball player. I made sure to point out that while *some* religions said it was okay to drink, the Bible said it was wrong. Which, of course, the Bible didn't say exactly, but I was giving the parents in the back of the room what they wanted to hear and what most of the teenagers present had already come to expect.

Take that, Catholic boy.

Oscar, for his part, didn't seem impressed. He spent the entirety of my message looking around the room, sizing up the girls. He never even saw Angela. She might have been an empty chair for all he cared. She beamed, though, as if he'd come riding in on a rainbow. The pudding sisters giggled as they cast glances at him, but he never looked back at any of them. I doubt he even knew their names.

I went home after work that night more excited than I had been in a while. As I lay in front of one of my pornos, I contemplated the mechanics of stage one of my plan. I'd need to get Brother Card as riled up as possible against Oscar. Let him do the hard work. Then, slowly, I'd work on Angela. Shower her with attention, praise, understanding.

I paused in the contemplation of the mechanics of my plan because the porn had reached its pivotal moment, and I reached a pivotal moment along with it. I went to the bathroom and cleaned up and then returned to my bed. I popped in another video and let it play as background music of sorts while I thought.

The Cards…

Even if I could get Angela to fall in love with me, what

about the parents? They wouldn't approve of their only begotten daughter being with the likes of me. I knew that. Do you doubt it? Do you think they would be happy to have me as a son-in-law? Don't bet on it. They wanted me where I was, leading the youth group, teaching the study lessons. They trusted me (at least Brother Card did), but they wanted me in my place. No one had ever wanted me to move freely about, doing what I wanted, chasing their daughters. Does that sound self-pitying? Maybe it is. Then again, the third fundamental truth of life is this: to 99.9% of the world you don't exist. I'm not being self-pitying when I say that because I'm talking about you. *You* do not exist to most of the rest of the world. How many people even know you're alive? Of those, how many care? Don't add it up if you're the type that gets easily depressed. Me, I'm not easily depressed. Never was. This nasty little world has always kind of amused me. I knew the world wanted me in my place—in a box on a shelf in the garage that they could take out when they needed it. That's why I became a youth minister in the first place, to serve a function. People would need me. (There's truth number four for you in case you're keeping count: how much people "care" about you is directly proportional to how much they actually need you.) They needed me to teach their zit-faced children about Jesus, to read the Bible to the kids and tell them, yes, it does say what your grandpappy told you it said. I was a tool and they cared for me like a tool, kept me clean and out of harm's way.

But now I wanted something. My love. I didn't know how to get rid of the Cards, but I hadn't ruled anything out.

I was thinking about all of this when someone knocked on my front door. I sprang up and turned off the television so quickly you would have thought my parents were coming through the door. After I got dressed, I hurried through the darkened living room to the front door.

When I opened the door, Angela was standing on my welcome mat. I said her name, and she started to cry.

Chapter Six

She wasn't wearing a coat, and when I pulled her to me and hugged her it was not a pleasant experience.

Leading her inside, I said, "You're freezing."

"I walked over," she said.

I sat her down on the couch and knelt next to her. A long strip of light from my bedroom gleamed across the hardwood floor of the living room, but she and I were in the dark. We were very close, but it wasn't an erotic moment. She smelled like cold wind and snot.

"Stay here," I said, as if she were going anywhere. I fetched some Kleenex, and she blew her nose. After throwing the tissue away and getting her a wool blanket, I went into the kitchen and microwaved some hot tea packets the Ladies Auxiliary had given me in a housewarming basket.

I paced the kitchen. Was now the time? This quick?

I shook my head. *You have to wait. You want to do this, but you have to wait it out. You don't know what's happened. If you pour it on too quick, it could scare her off. Take it easy.*

I noted my fortune in having just jerked off. Had I been humming along at full capacity when she showed up, I don't think I could have controlled what would have happened.

When the tea was ready, I took it in and gave it to her and sat down on the floor by her legs. Sweet, understanding guy.

"You seem better," I said.

And she did. She wasn't crying or shivering. She grinned and sipped her tea.

"Want to tell me about it?"

"Can I ask you a question?"

"I'd fill out the census for you," I said, but I thought, *Rein it in... Don't flirt.*

She smiled. "Have you ever been in love?"

"No," I said.

Leaning forward, holding the cup with both hands, she said, "I think I am."

"Why?"

"Why?"

"Yeah."

She frowned. "I don't know. I just feel love. Why haven't you ever been in love?"

I sighed. "I'm married to the work, I think. I want to serve God. Some people can do that without being married, some can't. Paul said that it was better for us not to marry, provided we could control our...urges. I've just always been able to control mine."

And Jesus, what a load of horseshit that was. Angela, my sweet untarnished goddess of light, thought about what I'd said for a while.

"Urges?" she finally said.

Here we go...

"Sexual," I explained. "But emotional, too. Are you having trouble with those?"

She shut her eyes and let the steam from the tea waft across her face. "I didn't run away from home, you know."

"I didn't figure you had."

"I just had to get out of the house."

"Is everything okay there?"

She shook her head and looked at me. "My father..."

"Is a good man," I said.

She took a sip of tea and said, "I know he is. He loves me and all, but he's such a ..." she tried to think of a word that wasn't a cuss word and came up with "...pedant. Do you know that word? I looked it up a couple of weeks ago for a paper I was doing in English. It means someone who's always bringing up little things to make themselves look smart because they don't know anything big. And that's what he is. That's why he's always quoting the Bible at whatever I say. No matter what point I try to make with him he brings up some scripture that proves I'm wrong."

"I thi—"

"And the thing is," she said, "I believe the Bible. I know it's God's word and whatever it says is right and all that, but *everything* I say can't be wrong."

"Of course not."

"Did he tell you about Oscar?"

"Oscar...the boy at church tonight?"

"Yeah."

"Is...Oscar the object of your affections?"

She took a long hard gulp of tea.

I said, "He seemed like a nice enough boy."

"He's just a boy at school. I think he's cute or whatever, but my father thinks I'm obsessed with him for some reason. He doesn't approve of him, so he doesn't like me having a stupid little crush on him."

"And why not?"

"Well, Dad doesn't want me to like anyone, but mostly it's because Oscar's Catholic."

"Surely it's not just that he's Catholic."

"Oh yeah," she said moving closer to the edge of the couch, "that's all it is. That he's Catholic. Now what kind of sense does that make?"

"I don't know," I said.

She frowned. It was as if she'd just heard herself talking about the love life of a movie star. "Plus, none of it matters anyway because…Oscar doesn't even know I'm alive, which, for some weird reason, my father doesn't believe. I mean, how is it his business who I like anyway?"

I mumbled out some more *your daddy loves you* business.

She shrugged. "I know, but he acts like I'm sinning by liking a guy. Oscar doesn't even know my name. It's crazy."

If she was uncomfortable sitting in the near dark she made no sign of it. She had warmed up now and even in the dim light I could see more color in her face. Angela. Such an ugly name, I think. Yet even now it sets me on fire. Angela. My angel.

"So what are you going to do, kid?"

She shook her head. "Go back home, I guess. My parents would kill me if they knew I was here."

"Why?" I laughed.

She frowned again, this time at my dimness. "At an older guy's house in the middle of the night? They'd die. My father would drop dead, and Mom would kill me, you, and then herself."

She laughed and seemed so much older all of the sudden. Was she used to sneaking out of the house? And she called me *an older guy*.

I shrugged it off. No Big Deal. "I don't think they'd mind but—"

"You're wrong," she said.

"But," I laughed, "maybe you shouldn't tell them you came over. No need worrying them about something that's not a problem."

She said, "I won't tell if you won't."

"I won't."

"Good. I'm sorry about showing up like this. You live closer than any of my friends, and my father keeps the only phone in the house in his bedroom."

"Gee, make me feel special why don't you?" I teased.

"No," she said with that pleading smile only a teenage girl can master. "It's not that. I think you're great."

"Thank you. I think you're pretty wonderful yourself."

She smiled. My angel.

"I should go," she said.

I said okay. We stood up and I walked her to the door. She touched the doorknob but turned around before she opened the door.

"I can't believe you've never been in love. You're the sweetest guy."

I smiled. "I'm waiting for the love of my life," I said.

She stared at me, opened her mouth to say something but then didn't. She smiled.

"What?" I asked.

"Nothing."

"C'mon, it was something."

She bit her lip. "Can I come back over here again?"

I had to take a deep breath just to find any breath at all. "Of course."

"I just like talking to you."

I looked into her eyes, and I didn't blink. Neither did she. I told her, "I like talking to you, too."

She blushed, turned and opened the door and slipped out into the night. I stood there for a moment. My hands trembled. Something inevitable was moving beneath the surface of my life, moving inside of me. I knew it, and it scared me, but I couldn't stop it.

• • •

After that first night, she started slipping out to see me.

I did very little on each occasion. Please believe that. She sat on the couch and talked and talked and I listened. Oh, I said things here and there, mostly affirming her view of the injustices visited upon her by her parents, but I didn't touch her one bit except for a hug to greet her and one to see her off. She came to think of me as a valuable friend and ally, certainly against her parents, but also against Oscar. It wasn't that he was mean to her. It was worse than that. He didn't know she existed. To make matters still harder for Angela, he would occasionally grin at her in the hall between classes, one of his big meaningless goofy grins, and every one of them was a bullet to her young heart.

Even though a lot of those early conversations were about Oscar, it was still fun to talk to her. She was, I suppose, the only girl I'd ever really sat and talked to for hours. All of it—her voice and her fears and her dreams and even her stupid love for that boy, all of it made me love her. Her self-esteem was lower than a slave's, but she could be funny and sweet, and everything about her fascinated me.

One night we were sitting and talking, and she told me, "I've never kissed a boy before."

"This sounds like the beginning of a question."

She chuckled. "Is that weird or what?"

"It's not so weird," I said.

"Why?"

"I think God wants us to wait until we find the right person. The one he intends for us."

She nodded, but then a wicked little smile crept onto her lips.

"Yeah. Well, that's not why I've been waiting, you know. It'd be nice if I *was* waiting for that, but I've been waiting because I have to. I ain't got a lot of options."

I wanted to lean over and kiss her then, of course, but I thought, *wait.*

"You'll do lots of kissing before you're done," I said. "The Lord shall provide."

She laughed and blushed and looked at her hands. When she looked back up at me, the space between us hung with the weight of what we weren't saying yet.

Finally, I broke it with a joke. We moved on to something else, but when she left that night she gave me a long hug. Then she stared at me for a while.

"You think I'll get to do some kissing?" she asked finally.

"I guarantee it," I said.

The next time she showed up things were different. We were both acting odd. She was nervous, but she was dressed up. She wore makeup and her hair smelled nice. She just looked so pretty.

My hormones were having an orgy. I swear to God, it was like I was sixteen. The difference, of course, was that I never got near a girl when I was sixteen.

We sat on the couch, just talking, and she kept looking at me. The lights were low, and it was late, and she just stared at me.

"Angela," I said.

She smiled. "I like when you say my name." Her face turned red; I could tell, even in the dark. I think I must have been the first man she'd ever flirted with. Her hands shook, and she held them tight on her lap.

"I like saying your name," I said.

She tried to smile and bit her lip at the same time. Poor thing.

"Angela?"

"Yes."

"Can I kiss you?"

She looked off and up and feigned thought. "Hmm." Then she smiled and we both laughed. "Yes," she said. When she said it, it was as if that little bastard Oscar had never been born. She never mentioned his name again.

I leaned over and took her trembling hand in my trembling hand and kissed her. She was the first girl I'd ever kissed. She is still the only girl I have ever kissed. I was at least as scared as she was.

After that we made out every time she came over. It progressed quickly into touching each other. Finally, one night it ended with us on my bed, our clothes half off and Angela pushing me away, "We shouldn't," she said. She covered her chest with one arm and her soft, white gut with the other arm.

"But we love each other," I said.

She said, "I love you more than anything, but we can't do this. What about the Lord?"

I took her hands slowly away from her torso and noticed a brown birthmark above her navel. "I want to marry you," I said.

She touched her bare chest as if she were short of breath. "Do you?"

"Of course, I do," I said. "Do you want to marry me?"

Her eyes filled with tears. "Yes, I do."

I rubbed her hand. "Then I think in God's eyes we are married. Marriage isn't some piece of paper, it's a holy bond. Two souls joined together in God."

She held my hand and looked down at it. "Yes," she said.

I squeezed her hands in mine. "Would you marry me right now?"

"Yes." She frowned. "But I'm too young."

I shook my head. "No," I said. "I don't mean 'let's go to

Vegas,' I mean *right now*, in the eyes of God. You, me and the Lord. The only three people that matter."

She chewed the inside of her cheek. "Yes. Yes, I'd do it right now."

We shut our eyes, she with her pale breasts bare as the noonday sun, me with a hard on, and I prayed a long and intricate prayer about the holy union of souls and the sacred covenant of marriage. You might think I was just trying to fuck her that night, trying at long last to lose my own virginity—and I won't say I wasn't—but I did also love her and I meant every word I said. I did want her to be mine. When I finished it, Angela was crying.

I said, "We're married."

I held her for a while and then we started kissing. Slowly I lowered her onto the bed.

"Hey," she said.

"What?"

She stared at me, looked me right in the eyes. I tried to look consumed by love instead of raging with lust.

Her brow was tight, her mouth crooked as she chewed on the inside of her cheek. She kept staring at me, *thinking*.

"What?" I said.

Still she stared and thought, and I didn't think it was going to happen, but then I saw the insecurity flood her eyes and she smiled painfully. And I knew I had her.

"You do love me, don't you? If we do this, you won't…"

"You're my wife," I said. "I love you. I will always love you."

She nodded. "I trust you," she said.

"And I love you," I said.

I had her at last.

• • •

After that, we didn't see each other for a few days. She was scared of me, I think. When she did finally come over she didn't want to have sex again, which hurt my feelings, of course.

"What if I get pregnant?" she said.

That certainly had never occurred to me. I didn't know a lot about that kind of thing. "Can't you take pills?"

She looked at me like I was crazy. "Where am I going to go to get birth control?" she said. "Why don't we just put a commercial on channel eleven?"

"There's no reason to be sarcastic," I said. "What about condoms? I could drive up to Black Bear and get some at Wal-Mart."

She asked, "They sell condoms at Wal-Mart?"

"Of course they do."

She chewed the inside of her cheek. "How do you know?"

I stared at her. "I've seen them there," I said. "I saw them one time in the pharmacy area."

She nodded, and I moved closer to her and took her hand. "I told you," I said, "there's only been you. There's only you, always."

I leaned forward to kiss her, but she pulled away.

"Please, baby," I said. "You're all I think about."

She stood up. "You think you're not all I think about?" she asked. "I can't read or watch TV. All I can do anymore is think about you. But it's all…happening so fast. It's happening really, really fast for me."

"I know," I said. I went to her and put my hands on her shoulders. "You're my wife. I can wait for you."

She grinned. "I should go," she said.

"Yeah."

"I'll see you tomorrow."

"Okay."

"Are you mad at me for not having sex with you?"

"No," I lied. "I just love you and want to express it to you. I don't take that lightly."

She said, "I don't either."

"Well," I said.

She sighed and kissed me. "You know I love you," she said. "I'm desperately in love with you. I cry at night thinking about you."

"Then make love to me," I said.

She smiled and hugged me, hugged me for a long time like a little girl. Then she said, "Let's make love."

Chapter Seven

Enter the villain.

The villain of the sad story of my miserable life is not, as I once thought, Oscar. Oscar, that little shit, would come back to haunt me later, but at the time he was simply the first brief obstacle I had to overcome. The swiftness with which I did away with Angela's love for him only confirmed that she was meant for me. The villain is not even Brother Card, who was a far more formidable opponent but was also, in the final analysis, a goddamn fool. No, the villain would turn out to be Timothy "Doolittle" Norris, the sheriff of our county.

I met him the night of our Valentine's Day banquet. The banquet was a tradition at Higher Living Baptist Church. It had been designed by some youth minister in years past as an alternative to more worldly get-togethers (read: get-togethers in which the kids might end up exchanging fluids). It was a lame event, to be sure. Essentially, it was a normal youth meeting with pink tinsel taped to the walls, a bowl of red punch and a couple of baskets of candy hearts. Our church had held onto the old Baptist belief—now defunct in many Baptist churches—that dancing was wrong, so instead we played some contemporary Christian pop music very low on a little jam box and the kids milled around and tried not to think about sex.

Everything was going well for me, and not just in the

area of Angela. The youth group, much to my surprise, was growing. We'd acquired several new kids into the fold (which did not include Oscar, who had not come back), and I'd even baptized a few.

The night of the banquet we had a good turnout. I was sitting in a corner listening to some saucer-eyed anorexic prattle on about her SAT scores, when Nick Hargrove, the youngest of our deacons, that "bright young man" Sister Card had introduced me to, brought over a burly, bowlegged man to meet me.

"Brother," Nick said, "this is Doolittle Norris."

"Good to know you," Norris said, extending his hand. His flushed cheeks and silver hair gave him a friendly, good old boy vibe, but he pretty well crushed my fingers. "I hear good things about your youth group."

"Thank you," I said. I had not heard good things about his sheriffing, but I didn't mention it. He'd narrowly won reelection the year before, and the gossip around church said his family supplied most of the county's marijuana and meth. I must have looked surprised to see him because he told me:

"My boy Tim is seeing one of the girls in your group. Figured I'd come check it out. Do a little, you know, hands-on parenting for a change."

Ah, I thought. I looked over and saw Tim, a quiet kid with droopy lips and jumbled teeth, sitting with a scrawny little brunette named Arial. Interestingly, my impressions of him had been that he was a very nice kid.

Doolittle Norris told me, "He likes it here a lot." He smiled when he said it, and I couldn't tell if he was making fun of me or his son.

"Do you attend church anywhere?" I asked pleasantly.

He smiled at—not with, but *at*—Nick. "Naw. Never had much use for it to be honest." Nick winced like he had an upset stomach, and Doolittle Norris jerked his head at the young deacon. "You know Nick here is my brother-in-law? Married my little sister. He kinda rescued Lacey from staying a Norris all her life."

"It's not that," Nick began. "Lacey still—"

"Don't matter," Doolittle Norris said, waving it off. He told me, "Nick and my sister don't much like it, the way I think about things. Some folks are into having people tell them what's right and wrong, and some ain't. I just never was."

"Yet you're the sheriff," Nick countered.

Norris shrugged. "Job's a job. Man's gotta eat." He looked at me. "Ain't that right, preacher?"

I started to stammer, but Nick jumped in before I could get a word out.

"I don't get your point," he said. "There's still a right and a wrong, and that right and wrong is set up by a god that is going to hold us accountable."

Norris shrugged again just to piss off Nick. "Ah, nobody knows what God thinks. I figure if God has anything he wants to say to me, he can go ahead and say it."

"Maybe he already did, in the Bible," Nick shot back. He rocked on his feet, hands at his sides. Nick liked to argue with people, and I could tell that unlike a lot of people—me for instance—he wasn't afraid of Doolittle Norris.

Norris laughed and swatted that away like Nick had asked him to dance. "You go on ahead and believe that if you want to, but I don't have time for it."

Nick's thick eyebrows were bunched together like they itched. "I can't believe you'd say these kinds of things in the Lord's house."

Norris laughed. "You want I should come in here and stoop and bow like a damn hypocrite? You think God would prefer me to lie?" He looked at me and smiled. "Sorry if that offends *you*, preacher." He seemed to be laughing at me when he said it.

Nick shook his head. He glanced around the room, already too irritated to have a civil conversation with his brother-in-law. I saw my chance to make some points with him by picking up the argument.

"I can't agree with you, of course," I told the sheriff. "The word of the Lord is as relevant today as it ever was, but you're honest and I admire your honesty. We'll be praying for you."

He chuckled, slipping his thick hands into the pockets of his jeans. "Well, you do that." He seemed amused by the entire conversation and jerked his head in the direction of his son. "Tim seems to like it here, and I guess it keeps him out of trouble."

"I'm glad to hear it," I said.

As I was speaking, Angela came in with the pudding sisters and looked over the banquet table. Someone had baked a chocolate cake and the girls began cutting off pieces from it. She didn't glance my way.

"Ain't that the preacher's daughter?" Doolittle Norris asked me.

"Yes," I said.

"Tim and her were sweethearts when they were in kindergarten."

Amazingly enough, this information made me jealous. I was destined, I suppose, to hate every man or boy who had ever spoken to her.

"That's funny," I said.

He smiled. His eyes were the color of polished steel, and they locked on me with a cold intensity. "She's got kinda big since then," he said, "but I guess you don't mind."

I stared back at him for a long difficult moment. Nick was oblivious to what was going on, and Doolittle Norris just smiled at me. I recovered myself and simply shrugged.

The sheriff said, "Well, I should be heading out, I guess."

Nick piped up, "Not yet, I hope. You'll miss what the youth minister here is telling your son every Wednesday."

The sheriff jeered, "I'm sure it's exciting stuff, but I got to go serve and protect. Y'all have a good evening." With that, he moseyed over to his son and announced he was leaving. The scrawny boy nodded, and Norris moseyed out the door.

Nick sighed and brushed some lint off his red polo shirt. "Well," he said, "that was Doolittle."

"Your family," I said.

He snorted. "Barely. Lacey barely speaks to them anymore."

"Why?"

Nick jerked his head in the empty space Doolittle Norris had occupied. "You can see for yourself. And Doolittle is, in some ways, just the tip of the iceberg."

"Really?"

He closed his eyes. "His mother…"

"Mrs. Norris, I presume."

Nick looked at me. "Mrs. Norris indeed. I don't want to be… Look, I don't want to be unchristian about it. I would never say that anyone was beyond God's reach. But Mrs. Bertie Mae Norris, is…the only completely evil person I've ever met."

"That's incredible. Lacey is so sweet."

"And she's as different from her mother as the sun is from the moon. Lacey's a woman full of the Holy Ghost and she's a beautiful soul." Nick cocked his head and grinned sadly. "But she's had to struggle to overcome her past. The same way a lot of us have."

"Including you?"

Nick looked around the room like he hadn't heard the question. Finally he said, "My dad was…" And he let it die.

"I didn't know that about your father," I said. "I wouldn't have guessed it."

Nick's face pinched up soberly. "Oh yes. My old man was a piece of work. Alcohol and women. Never home. It's like he studied to be the classic example of a bad father. The only good thing he ever did was leave my mother and me when I was about twelve. Years later, when I met Lacey's mother, I recognized the type." He waved his hand. "Sort of. My father was terrible at being my father, but Bertie Mae is…bad. The whole family is bad news."

"They're a legend around here," I said.

"They should be," he said. "It's like the Arkansas mafia or something. Word is, they control most of the meth labs in the Ozarks. They cook it up there and ship it down here. That's the rumor, anyway. I have no firsthand knowledge of that, of course, but the family is certainly involved in criminal enterprise and has been for years."

"How's Lacey feel about it?"

He shrugged. I could tell he didn't like going into those kinds of places. Nick was Mr. Get Things Done. He didn't like this kind of talk.

"Just keep praying," I finally said.

"Absolutely. And let it go after that." He clapped his hands. "I think I'll go get some punch."

After he'd gone off, I milled around talking to parents and kids, watching different kids pairing up, watching Angela and her friends giggling like fools in the corner. I rarely spoke to her in public anymore and she rarely spoke to me, although when we were forced into a situation where we had to talk in public she was as cool as a spy about it. This, of course, filled me with desire. A few times that night we met eyes across the room and smiled and then dropped it. I knew we had to be careful in public. Doolittle Norris had shaken me a bit with his insinuations.

The banquet wound down with a mass exit of kids and parents at nine-thirty. Angela and her friends looked ready to drift out a little later, so I went up to them.

"You all leaving?" I asked.

Angela nodded and smiled. "Yeah. We're going over to Mary's to watch movies." She was dressed very proper that night, with moderate make-up on, her hair back in a ponytail, gray sweater and knee-length skirt.

"Sounds like fun."

They all smiled and nodded as they inched toward the door. Angela narrowed her eyes a little as if to say, *Don't be obvious. Don't embarrass me.* I knew then for sure that the pudding sisters didn't know anything about our late nights.

"Well, have fun," I said.

One by one, the other families collected themselves and left until I was alone in the church. The ladies had done the dishes and the men had folded up the chairs, so all I had to do was go through the building, turn off all the lights and lock up for the night.

It took me longer than usual to lock up the building, but when I stepped outside I was surprised to see a truck idling beside my car in the otherwise empty parking lot.

The driver's side window of the truck rolled down and there was Doolittle Norris with a cheek swollen with tobacco, a spit-cup on the dash. A book on tape played loudly: something about the invasion of Normandy.

"Hello," I said, with an unmistakable quiver in my voice.

"Howdy, Brother Webb," he said. "You ready to talk about the preacher's daughter?"

Chapter Eight

Doolittle Norris was smiling, smiling like a villain, glorying in my squirming.

"What do you mean?" I asked. Might as well fight it for a little while.

"Climb in," he said, nodding at the passenger side. The book on tape droned on about giant waves sweeping men into the sea.

"It's a little late for me," I said.

He shrugged. "It ain't so late. I bet you Mister Brother Card is still up." He took the cup off the dash and spit and scratched his nose.

"He probably is," I said.

"Then get in and let's you and me chew the fat for a little while."

My scalp itched and my back felt chilled, but I walked around the truck and climbed in. It was a huge tank of a thing, with a dashboard full of lights and a long bench seat. It felt as if he and I were in different time zones. Norris slid the spit cup into a plastic holder by his knees and backed the truck out. Then he gunned it to the edge of the parking lot, let some cars pass, and flew out the opposite direction toward Fenton Road. There was a little American flag on his radio antenna fluttering sharply in the wind. We sped past gas stations and houses and long, lonely stretches of trees, and all the while the man on the tape talked about American soldiers being gunned down before they even got to the beach.

"Could we turn that off?" I asked.

Norris shrugged and turned it off. When he reached over to hit the button on the tape player I noticed for the first time there was now a gun clipped to his belt. He noticed me notice it and smiled.

"Last line of defense between me and the bad guys," he said.

"What's the first line?"

"Pure heart," he said. "And the right intentions." He spit into his cup. "And the law, of course. Can't forget the law."

"What do you want?" I asked. I meant to sound tough, but I sounded weak and stupid.

Norris pulled a nasty handkerchief from a pocket and dabbed at his mouth. "Right. Straight to the point. That's the way I like it myself."

We passed the Dyess aluminum plant and Norris said, "See, here's the thing: I drive around town a lot at night. Keeping vigil, you know. Protecting and serving into the wee small hours of the morning. It's mostly boring. Occasionally, you run off some niggers who drift out of their part of town into ours. Occasionally, you rough up some mouthy teenagers. But mostly, you just ride around. That's why I listen to my books. Gives me something to think about on the lonely nights."

I wanted to say, *The way I hear it you're never bored. I hear you spend your time micro-managing the drugs coming into the county. I hear the people you beat up are the drug dealers who aren't giving you a piece of their action.* I didn't say anything, of course.

"I'm watchful, though," he said. "For instance, one night I saw this girl walking down Church Street. Teenager. Kind of on the thick side. So I'm about to pull over and talk to her but before I can, what does she do?"

He waited until I said, "I don't know."

"It's funny you don't know, because she went to your house. So I'm thinking, that's the house old lady McCarthy gave Tim's church. Youth minister's house. And so, being concerned for the wellbeing of what looked to me to be a minor, I hung around. Waited for an hour or so—during which time, by the way, the lights never come on in the house. Darkness. Then, finally, she came out and I followed her home. I drove past her, waited behind houses, stuff like that and she never noticed. Went straight to the preacher's house."

"It's not what you think," I said.

"Course not," he said. "I got a dirty mind unwashed by the blood of the Lamb. I know that. But I kept watch the next night, and the next—made it part of my nightly rounds—and she went back a lot."

Okay. So here's the thing: I know that earlier I might have made it sound as if she'd only come back to see me a few times. I suppose it was more than that. Looking back on it now, I think it was more than that. But the truth is nothing bad was happening there. We were in love, after all.

Most people wouldn't accept the truth, though. I knew that. And I knew Norris wouldn't accept the truth. So I lied, and he just laughed when I explained the lie, explained that she and I were friends and that we were only talking about problems with her father and school and life. He didn't believe me at all.

"Sure. Sure, I know," he said as we slid back onto Church Street. "You were doing your duties as a minister, late at night, in the dark, with a chubby, underage piece of ass. I completely believe you, but the question is: will her daddy?"

I sulked in the corner of his big truck and didn't say anything. What was there to say to that? I would lose my job. And, if they could, the Cards would have me put in jail for statutory rape, a jail run by Doolittle Norris.

Norris drove past my house ("Now, that *is* your house, right?") and swung by the Cards' house as well. He slowed down, grinning at me in the rearview mirror. When we were out of the neighborhood, he cut through the Wal-Mart parking lot a few blocks away and headed back to the church. "Of course, we could avoid all that," he said. "But you'd have to do something for me."

"What?" I asked.

He nodded. "That's better. You don't need to bullshit me about the girl. I don't care. She's...what? Sixteen, seventeen. Back not all that long ago, she'd already have a kid or two. Some places in the world they still marry them off at fourteen, fifteen."

"What do you want from me?" I asked belligerently. "I don't have much money, but I can give you a little. Just tell me what you want and leave me the hell alone."

He swung the truck over to the side of the road and threw it into park. I lurched forward and thumped my head against the windshield. By the time I'd regained my balance, he'd unholstered his gun and pointed it at my mouth.

I plastered myself to the door and clawed at the seat with my fingernails. His face was a sick orange from the dashboard. "Real quick now, let's have a clarification session. You're a fucking weasel, and I own you. You're my fucking weasel. You get tough with me, or fuck around with me, and I'll skip sending your ass to jail. I'll put a bullet in your skull and stick you out in the woods under a rock."

"Okay," I pleaded.

"You believe me now?"

"Yes, sir. Please. Please just tell me what you want."

He stared at me for a while and then holstered his gun, put the truck in drive and said, "Good. Don't want us to misunderstand each other." He smiled again and reached for his spit cup. "I need you to do a little favor for me."

I peeled myself off the door and settled somewhat into the seat. *Jesus*.

"You know who Mrs. Eleanor Dyess is?" he asked.

"No."

"Old lady in your church?"

I shook my head, although I wasn't really trying to remember. I was still thinking about his gun pointed at me.

"Course not," he said. "You're too busy banging teenagers after church to notice. Mrs. Dyess is the widow of Fred Dyess who owned the aluminum plant out on Fenton Road. Now she owns it. Or did."

"What do you mean?"

"She died a couple of hours ago. Cancer."

Then I remembered Brother Card trying to tell me about her the first night I had dinner at his house. I wished I'd been paying attention. "I remember her now," I said. "She's been sick since I got here. I never met her though."

"That's understandable, you being so involved with the youth and all," he said.

I didn't reply to that.

"Here's the point," he said. "Mrs. Dyess left something very important with your friend the preacher."

"With Brother Card?"

"One and the same. And he's got this important document at his house."

"How do you know that?"

He shrugged. "The old lady was a religious kook. She had a falling out with her kids years ago, and the only person she trusted was Brother Card. The lawyer involved in the distribution of Mrs. Dyess's estate is a…family friend. He was present when your would-be father-in-law put this document in the bottom drawer of his desk at home."

"But how do you know it's still there? He might have moved it."

Doolittle Norris shook his head. "It's there. There's no reason for him to have moved it. Not until tomorrow morning, anyway."

"But—"

"Stop talking," he groaned. "Jesus Christ. All you have to worry about is going in there tonight and getting it out. Simple burglary. According to the state, you're already legally a rapist. You can't step up to a little B&E?"

I shook my head. "But how would I even go about it? I've never done anything like this before."

"You're about to learn," he said.

"What is it, this document?" I asked. "What am I looking for?"

He let that hover in the air between us as he pulled into the church parking lot and stopped at my car. "In his office at home… Bottom drawer on the right hand side. Where he keeps his important church documents. It's a manila envelop with DYESS written across it in marker. You can't miss it. I'll call you tomorrow night." He jerked his head at the door. "Now get out."

I opened the door and climbed out. I felt sluggish and exhausted.

"Hey," he said.

"Yeah." I stopped with my hand on the door.

He stared at me for a long time. "Come tomorrow night you'd best have that goddamn envelope."

"I understand."

"I'm not talking about going to jail on a statutory rape charge."

"I understand."

"Good," he said. "Get to work."

Chapter Nine

I waited until his truck disappeared into the distance before I dragged myself back into the church. I was too smart not to sneak into Brother Card's office and check through his files. I was hoping like hell he had moved that envelope to the church. His door was unlocked, and I searched his office thoroughly. It was all for nothing, though, and that meant there were no options left to me but to drive home and get ready to burgle the Cards' home. On the way there, I swung by the hospital to see if Brother Card's car was in the parking lot. It wasn't. I assumed he had to have been there when the old lady died, done his consoling, and gone home for the night.

When I got home, I went to my room and dropped onto the bed and thought things over. I was still looking for a way out.

But what could I do but go into the house and try to get that envelope? I suppose I could have slinked out of town, disgraced, or maybe I could have even attempted to explain things to the Cards. But it wouldn't have done any good. I needed to stay, to be close to Angela, and to do that I had to get Doolittle Norris off my back. If it meant crawling around in the dark, so be it. If they caught me, I'd be screwed. I'd lose my job for sure, but at the very least I'd have Norris in my corner when they called the cops. The risks were huge, but the only other option held nothing but grim certainties.

I picked myself up and changed into the darkest clothes I had. *Jesus*, I thought as I was changing, *this is crazy*. I'd never done anything like this before, never snuck around at night, never broken into a house. But as I set myself to doing it—slipping a small flashlight and utility knife in my pockets—there was a slight change in my attitude. Despite the fear, or maybe because of it, I felt wide awake, and I was hyperaware of my skin and bones. I felt alive.

It was cold out, of course, but I was too nervous to feel it much. Through the shadows of my backyard, I crept along the edge of the woods, just behind the houses on Church Street. Every backyard I passed scared the hell out of me, but no one was out. A couple of dogs barked at me, but those damn dogs were always barking at something. The neighborhood was asleep. I stayed just inside the shadows and trees, and took my time with it. When I got to the end of our block I had to cross the open road that intersected Church Street. I took it at a light trot and entered the woods on the other side. From there, I crossed a few lightly timbered acres and arrived at the edge of the Cards' neighborhood. I crept along behind houses and stayed as much as I could in the woods. The houses were dark; the neighborhood was in bed and sleeping soundly. From there on out, I didn't even run across a barking dog. When I got to the back of the Cards' house, I was not surprised to find all the lights were off.

Behind me, the woods seemed to take a breath. Branches creaked, and pine needles scoured the night air. I crouched down and scanned the yard. There was a good bit of space between the Cards' house and their nearest neighbor. I tried remembering the setup of the house. The living room window was on the left and looked out onto a dozen-or-so feet of grass and a six foot wooden fence. The fence seemed to exist only as a demarcation line between the properties of Card and his neighbor.

Card had told me once that his office didn't have a workable window because he didn't want to be distracted in prayer. That made the living room the best place to scope out the inside of the house, so I slid up to the window and peeked inside. The sill was a little high, but I could see okay. The room was dark, of course, but I could make out the couch and the large television draped in shadows. The house was asleep. I snuck around to the back door and tried it. Locked, of course. I went back to the living room window and tried it. It wasn't locked.

My bladder suddenly felt as if it might burst. My scalp tightened. Going around to the back of the house, I looked for something to stand on. I found Brother Card's chopping block by the woodpile and put it under the window. Then I eased up the window as quietly as I could, sliced open the bottom of the screen, and pulled the screen frame out. I dropped it on the grass and struggled to pull myself up and through the window. It was difficult to do it quietly, and I don't exactly have catlike stealth, but I lowered myself onto the living room carpet without making too much noise.

The house seemed hot after walking through the frigid night air, and I crouched there beside the window for a while letting my fingers and toes thaw out. I wasn't really cold until that moment, and then I was shivering in the warmth of the Cards' home.

The house had that fragile silence all places get at night. Every move I made seemed magnified a thousand times. When I finally picked myself up and started to cross the room, I felt as if I were walking over a sheet of glass.

From the kitchen the refrigerator hummed, but otherwise the house lay silent. Creeping past the kitchen, I inched down the carpeted hallway. I took each step as if the floor might break. I passed the bathroom door, which was closed. Beneath the door, no light. The office door was open, and I went in. Shut the door. Delicately. Turned on the flashlight. Across the room to the desk. Crouched behind it. Eased open the bottom drawer. Delicately. And there it was.

It was a long manila envelope with DYESS written in magic marker. I slipped it into my coat and was raising myself up when I heard a toilet flush and the bathroom door open.

Dropping down again, I knocked over a paperweight on Card's desk and the goddamn thing hit the carpet with a thud. I fumbled with the flashlight but clicked it off.

Then there was silence.

Loud silence.

Nothing.

I didn't breathe.

Then there was the sound of movement, the sound of weight moving away from me and toward the kitchen.

I eased up just a little and saw nothing, of course, but the door of the office. It was possible that the toilet flush had obscured the paperweight. Whoever it was in the bathroom might not have heard it. They might not have seen the light.

My body was tense—but not in a useless way. I was coiled, ready. I wiped sweat from my face and felt more sweat drip from my armpits.

I waited.

Every second weighed a thousand pounds.

I kept waiting.

There was no sound coming from the kitchen. Nothing.

Were they on the phone to the cops? Doubtful. You'd investigate a sound like the paperweight before you'd dial up the cops. Had they seen the light? Had they passed by and gone on to bed? It was possible I'd misheard and just thought they were going to the kitchen.

The longer I waited the more likely that seemed.

One thing was for sure: I couldn't just wait. The longer I waited, the more chance I had of getting caught. The office did have a small window, but Card, more concerned with books and solitude than the view of his backyard, had obscured it with two heavy bookshelves. To make matters worse, the shelves had long ago sunk into the carpet. Even if I didn't care about the noise, I couldn't get those shelves out of the way to get out the window.

Nothing was happening outside that door. No whispers. No patter of feet. No dialing of the phone. Nothing.

I had to move.

I eased up and crept, weightlessly it seemed like, to the door and listened. Listened hard. But there was nothing, goddamn it. I'm telling you, there was no sound. I decided to go for it. If one of the Cards were up and about, I'd just have to run for the window. There was no other option.

I eased the door open, and it made the slightest sucking noise, like a vacuum being released, and I opened it wider. The hinges squeaked. I paused.

Nothing.

I stepped into the hall. The bedrooms were at the end, across from each other, and both doors were open slightly, but everything was dark and quiet.

I crept down the hall toward the living room. Past the bathroom. The door was open, and a little nightlight shone alone in the dark.

Inching along, I passed the darkened kitchen. Quietly. I was almost to the living room window when I realized there was someone in the kitchen watching me.

Chapter Ten

It was Sister Card.

She stood there frozen. Wearing a long t-shirt and pink ankle-high socks. And holding that goddamn butcher knife. When I turned, she tried to scream but nothing came out. She looked so absurd trying to scream I could have laughed, but I didn't.

I rushed her. I didn't have a plan. I wasn't thinking. I just did it. I leapt at her and punched her in the face. I'd never struck anyone before, and when the impact hurt my hand, it startled me. Sister Card toppled over. The poor woman never even raised the knife. I guess she was just too scared. I don't think she ever even realized it was me.

I wrested the knife away from her. Then I stuck it in her chest and stomach and throat. I did it over and over without thinking until she stopped kicking and the scream which never did emerge from the back of her throat finally bubbled away and she was dead.

And that was it.

I was a murderer. The whole thing probably took less than two minutes. Sister Card had lived for forty-odd years—was born, grew up, fell in love, got married, had sex, made babies, gathered friends, lost friends…and in two minutes I'd murdered her.

I knelt there beside her body, feeling the linoleum sticky with blood beneath me, and looked at her.

Dead.

I was thinking about that when Brother Card screamed. He'd heard us thumping around in the kitchen and had run up the hall to find his wife dead on the kitchen floor next to me. His hair stuck out like a wild man's and he wore a plain orange t-shirt and white briefs. He lunged at me, screaming. He *did* know it was me. I could see the recognition—clouded by horror as it was—on his face. He must have thought he was in a nightmare, or maybe hell. He slipped a little in his wife's blood as he came at me, and I stuck the knife into his throat, going through his Adam's Apple and up into his head. It happened quickly, quicker than with Sister Card, although Brother Card made more noise. He screamed, a high pitched, almost female scream, but the knife tore up his throat too bad. He tried to strangle me, but I just kept pushing on the knife, trying to get it up to his brain, and the handle cracked but I kept pushing. He kept trying to get at me and although he didn't know it, the more he tried to get me the more he helped me, and the whole time I kept pushing. Finally, he couldn't take it and started clawing at his throat, but by then it was too late. He was choking on the knife. I kept pushing. And finally he stopped moving.

When it was all over, I lay covered in their blood, shaking like a newborn baby. I pulled myself off the floor and slumped onto a kitchen chair and looked at them. Brother Card lay at his wife's knees, still clutching his throat. Sister Card stared at the ceiling. Blood soaked everything like someone had dumped a bucket of it on us.

I don't know how long I sat there. Too long to be smart, I suppose, but nothing happened. I just stared at them, and they just stayed dead.

"Jesus," I said finally.

I said it as a curse, of course, but when it came out, it just sort of sat there: Jesus. I looked at the Cards. Nothing. They were a bloody pile of meat and bone, just like me. I was sitting on a wooden chair at a wooden table someone had carved out of a tree. Everything seemed heavy and solid. Even the name: Jesus. All of a sudden it seemed like there was a god. It was as if I'd always been a little off center and someone had bumped me and, just for a second, I was on center and everything seemed thick and hard and real.

I shook that out of my head and got up. I had some important things to think about. Focus. What if Card had made a phone call before he came in and the police were coming? I went to the front window and parted the blinds. Nothing. The street was empty and quiet. I turned around, and then I saw something that made me smile. I walked over to the couch and picked up the cordless phone resting against a cushion. The only phone in the house.

After making sure all the windows and blinds in the house were closed, I strolled back to the bathroom and turned on the light. Underneath a damp red sheen, my face was pale. I ran some warm water and washed up, and pink water swirled down the drain and splattered on the sides of the sink. I looked in the mirror again, and my face was still bloody. The more I looked at the blood, which an hour before had been running through their veins and soaking their muscles, the more disgusting it became. I stripped off my bloody clothes and got into the shower.

Maybe taking a shower right then sounds crazy to you. Maybe it was, and maybe I am crazy. I don't know. What I do know is that I have never been more rational than right after I killed the Cards. It was late and the neighbors were probably asleep. I had no reason to think the cops were on their way, and I calculated that staying and showering was a smarter risk to take than traipsing back through the woods soaked in DNA. Better to wash as much of the evidence down the drain.

Taking that quick shower, I was as objective as I could be. It was like working out an equation. I ran the water hot and scrubbed off good, washing with soap and shampoo. Once the initial shock of killing the Cards had subsided, I was just a man trying to solve a problem. I didn't have any experience with this sort of thing, of course. I hadn't planned to kill the Cards, and I had made no preparations for it. I had to improvise, and I needed to do it quickly. By the time I was done with the little shower, I had it all figured out.

I dried off and went into the Cards' bedroom and put on a pair of Brother Card's slippers, some khaki shorts and his red *Ask Me About Jesus* t-shirt. Then I dug out his darkest clothes: a pair of black dress shoes, black slacks, dark brown sweater and a black blazer. I lay them on the bed, and I walked back to the kitchen. It was a gruesome sight. The Cards were exactly as I had left them, their eyes open, vacant and rubbery-looking. It was bizarre, really, how they were no longer people. They were objects on the floor. They didn't have breath or thoughts or a future. They were just objects. Messy objects. The whole place was covered in blood: dried blood and sticky blood and wet blood.

I went out to the garage and rummaged around until I found a plastic container of gasoline three quarters full. I carried it into the kitchen and set it on the table.

Then I dug out Sister Card's salad tongs, went down the hall to the bathroom and plucked my bloody clothes off the floor like they were a science experiment. As much as possible, I tried to avoid any blood. I took out the envelope crumpled in my jacket. It looked like hell, but it wasn't bloody. I left it with the clean clothes in the bedroom. Then I went back to the kitchen, threw the bloody clothes on top of the Cards and walked back down the hall to Angela's room. It was what I'd thought it would be: girly, smelling of her perfume. There was a writing desk with a pile of school books. A big bed with a white comforter and a pink skirt. The walls were covered in pictures of river otters and dolphins, a map of the world and a poster of a shitty Christian rock band called By His Stripes.

I opened her chest-of-drawers, went through her underwear, looked at her yearbooks (her photo was glum and made me sad, but there was a crown of hearts around Oscar's photo and I threw the book down) and searched through her closets. I was hoping to find a diary of some kind, but she didn't seem to have one.

I pulled the comforter off the bed, turned off the light and carried the comforter back down the hall to the chamber of horrors. I doused the Cards in gasoline but made sure I didn't use too much too quickly and didn't splash any on myself. I ran a line of gasoline down the hall, splashing some in the bathroom on the dry towels and running a line into both bedrooms. I finally ran out of gas pouring it around the Cards' bed. I looked under the kitchen sink and found some lighter fluid and went into Brother Card's office and sprayed his papers and books, anything that would burn well. I did the same thing all over again in the living room, making sure to spray some on the carpet and sofa.

Then I stripped off the t-shirt and shorts and changed into the darker clothes I'd laid out on the bed. I slid the Dyess envelope into the pocket of the blazer and walked carefully back down the hall. I stuffed Angela's comforter in the oven, soaking it with the last of the lighter fluid. The matches were in a drawer under the microwave. After I'd turned on the oven and the range, I struck a match and dropped it on the Cards.

Chapter Eleven

I took my time getting home, staying further back in the woods than I had before, and trying to keep cool. The streets were quiet and I was quiet with them. I knew better than to rush home. Keep cool.

Lying on my bed when I got home, I looked over the papers in the manila envelope for a few minutes before I tucked them away. I'm not much of a hand at legal documents to begin with, and my damn hands kept shaking, but the papers were pretty straightforward. It was a copy of a will, and it looked to me as if Mrs. Dyess had turned over ownership of the aluminum plant to the church. I couldn't concentrate very well, but that was what I got from what I read. I also saw the words *in excess of four million dollars*.

It was about what I figured. It looked like Mrs. Dyess's lawyer was a guy named Vandover Norris. I assumed he was the "family friend" that Doolittle had mentioned. I tried to reason my way through it, tried to figure out what the Norrises were up to, but I couldn't focus. I put the papers in my trunk in the closet under my pornos and, exhausted, flung myself onto the bed and tried to sleep. I was too nervous, though. My mind raced.

What I'd just done seemed like it had happened in a former life, as if it were some ancient, buried memory instead of something that had happened a few hours before. But it *had* happened. Two people were dead. Two people who were living were now not living because I'd decided—in a very off hand manner I might say—to take their lives.

The full importance of this didn't really occur to me until later on, but as I lay there in the small, quiet hours of the morning—knowing that not all that far away the Cards' house was a burning hell—I couldn't get it off my mind. I wasn't racked with guilt, understand. I wish I could say I was, but I wasn't. The Cards hadn't deserved to die any more than most people do, but I hadn't killed them because they deserved it. It was simply what had happened. And I thought about it on that level. I just couldn't quite believe it had actually happened. Maybe it had been easy because I'd never liked Sister Card and she'd never liked me. Maybe I was just scared. Why do these things happen, anyway? I don't know. They just do. If there is a god, I suppose these kinds of things must be part of him and his big master plan. Maybe they're his idea of a joke, the overlapping ironies of his inexhaustibly complex nature. If there's not a god, then this kind of wickedness is simply a facet of the human psyche, some glitch we haven't worked out yet and probably never will.

I tried to think about Angela, but she started to seem small compared to what I'd done for her. That made me angry for a moment, but I let it pass. No use getting mad at her. She hadn't done anything. Just then she was at a friend's house, sleeping soundly probably, with no idea her parents were dead. Silly of me to get mad at her.

In a way—and I'm fully aware that you may have trouble making this leap, but do me and favor and try—it seemed like some real good might come from what I'd done. I mean, in a sense, things for me had just improved. The Cards had always been the only real obstacle between me and Angela.

Except maybe Oscar, but he was just some pathetic little basketball player. Had she ever even loved him? I doubt it. Love at that age, what is it really? Nothing but hormones colliding with insecurity in a limited pool of options.

I actually loved her.

Or I thought I did. Many people would say I didn't. But let's put it this way: I killed for her. I didn't plan on it, but when the challenge came, I took it. I actually murdered people for her, like Abraham ready to sacrifice Isaac to prove he loved god. God himself demanded that kind of love. How demented could it be? I wasn't desperate after I killed the Cards, I was glad. I was locking it in. No matter what, I would be joined with Angela forever. She would need me now more than ever.

The more I thought about her, though, the more that something tugged at me. The last obstacle.

Doolittle Norris. I didn't want to think too much about him or about our inevitable confrontation. Thinking too much will always mangle your mind. I needed to be clear when I saw him. I decided not to think about him.

Which left me with nothing but the really Big Questions, the moral implications of what I'd done. Well, who wants to think about that shit? I watched a porno instead and finally fell to sleep.

The doorbell rang about three hours later. It was early, and sunlight was just beginning to splinter the night sky. When I opened the door Doolittle Norris shoved his way in, threw me to the floor, and slammed the door shut behind him. He stalked over to the curtains and peered outside.

Then he spun around.

"What the fuck happened?"

I motioned at the door. "Did anyone see you come in?"

He glared at me like I was a fool. "No. Do you think I want people seeing me come in here right, now?"

"No," I said. "I don't think you do." I couldn't help but smile when I said it.

He stared at me for a long moment and took a step back and leaned against the wall. He crossed his arms. "Well," he said, "you little motherfucker. You little piece of shit."

I shrugged and pushed myself off the floor.

"Care to sit down?" I said.

"No."

"Then let's get down to it," I said. "I have what you want. I've done something for you, now you can do something for me."

"Killing the preacher and his wife and burning their fucking house to the ground wasn't my idea. That was yours."

"True. That's why you're called an *accomplice*," I said. "I bet when they give me the lethal injection, you don't do more than ten or fifteen years. But I doubt you want that. I doubt you want to go to jail at all."

Violence simmered in his eyes and his ruddy cheeks were hot with blood, but Norris hadn't become the criminal he was by beating the shit out of people when it didn't benefit him. He stared at me and said, "Be careful with what you say."

"I will," I said. "But you can see I'm right. I'm sitting on a few million dollars for you. However you plan to get it, I'm the key. I have the will. You need it, and I have it."

"What makes you think I need it now? I could just say it burned up in the fire."

I shook my head. "C'mon, don't treat me like that. We both know why you're here. If you didn't need me, I'd be in jail or dead already. You can't throw me in jail because you know I'll name you as an accomplice, and you don't want to kill me because I have the key to old lady Dyess's money."

He did. He stared at me and thought, and I could tell he knew I was right. "Where's the envelope?" he asked.

I grinned at him disappointedly. He shrugged.

"So," he said, "you've got it stashed away somewhere. Now what do you want?"

"Two things. Not big things either. First, I want you to take care of this little mess we have."

He ran his hand through his hair and rubbed his eyes. "It's a hellish nightmare over there."

"Can you pass it off as an accident?"

"Christ, no. It looks like a murder scene. I'm not the only one there, you know. Anyone who sees it can tell it's a murder scene." His face screwed up in revulsion the more he thought about it. "Accident! Are you out of your mind, you sick bastard? There's a guy with a fucking knife in his skull." He shook his head. "I can't pass that off as an accident."

I shrugged. "So it's a murder. Investigate it like a murder then. But you know where it can't lead."

He pursed his lips and weighed the chances of success. "It's not going to be as easy as you think."

"That's your problem now," I said.

I don't know why I was needling him, but he didn't respond to it at all. He only scratched his chin and asked, "What's your second condition?"

"That you see to it Angela stays here in town."

"Angela…"

"The preacher's daughter."

"Oh," he said, stretching the syllable out. "The preacher's daughter." He shook his head and rubbed the bridge of his nose.

"She's got an aunt in town," I said. "See to it she stays

here. I don't want them sending her down to Texas to stay with her grandparents. Say she needs to stay here. Throw some police jibberish at them."

"And then what?"

I shrugged. "As soon as the case closes, you get your papers."

He pushed himself off the wall and said, "I'll be in touch with you. Don't you call me. Expect me to show up."

"Okay."

He nodded and went to the window and peered out. Then, without saying anything else, he slipped out into the breaking dawn.

Looking back on it, I think he'd already decided to kill me.

Chapter Twelve

The next few days were consumed with managing the reaction to the Cards' deaths. The chairman of the deacons called me crying in the early hours of the morning of the murders to let me know what had happened. He was an old man, but I don't think he'd ever experienced anything like this.

I reacted like he would expect me to react. I was daunted, shaken, horrified, but brave and ready for what lay ahead, assuring him that we needed prayer and supplication before the Lord now more than ever. I asked him to arrange a meeting with the deacons for that night.

"The important thing for us in a time like this," I said, "is to stay close to the Lord and close to each other."

"I couldn't agree more," he said.

"How many people have you talked to?"

"Just a few. Nick Hargrove called me and let me know."

The bright young man was moving forward already. It figured. "How did he find out?" I asked.

"Well, his brother-in-law, as you may know, is the sheriff," the chairman told me.

"I didn't get the impression they were on good terms."

"I don't believe they are," the chairman said, "but I believe the sheriff felt compelled to tell his sister that her pastor was dead."

"I see. And you didn't talk to too many others before you called me," I said.

"I made one or two calls, but I assume the word is all over by now."

"That's a safe bet," I said. "That's one very good reason for the senior staff and the deacons to meet."

"Absolutely," he said. "I'm sure Nick will feel the same."

After I hung up, I made the rounds. I went by the music minister's home, went by the home of the Senior Adult minister, and stopped by the church to help the secretary field calls for a few hours. Then I went by and saw Nick Hargrove.

The bright young man had a nice house in a new subdivision up by the school. There was a new car shining under a basketball goal in the driveway. As I walked up to his front door, I could see the edge of a swimming pool jutting out from behind the house.

Nick's wife answered the door. Lacey Hargrove was a rosy-cheeked blonde with a cute overbite, but she had a crying baby on her hip and she looked grim.

"He's in his office," she said.

I tried to see the similarity between her and Doolittle Norris, but there wasn't any. Nothing about her marked her as a Norris. Whether that was genetics or the work of the Holy Ghost is anyone's guess.

She led me through the house, and I watched her ass as she went down the hall. The baby stopped crying and watched me watch its mother's ass. I shrugged.

"Nick," she said, tapping on the door.

Nick sat at his desk and turned when we came in. He stood up. "Hey there." He kissed his wife on the cheek and shook my hand.

"Could you take her?" Lacey asked.

Nick grimaced but took the kid without a word. Lacey left. "Have a seat," he said.

I sat in a hard-backed chair by the desk, and we exchanged some words of remorse about the Cards. I went on autopilot and said everything you're supposed to say. While he talked, I looked around the office a little.

It was neat and clean. There were two bookshelves full of history, religion and politics. Paintings of flaxen-haired angels and sun-kissed clouds hung along the walls, and above his desk, next to a partial list of Southern Baptist missionaries, a tack-filled map of the world gave Nick his view of the big picture.

He stopped talking and held the baby to his chest. The kid looked ready to cry.

Nick smiled when he saw me looking at the kid. "She likes me. It's funny," he said. "She's more at ease with me than her mother." He shook his head. "Odd."

"It is," I said.

"Have you thought about kids?" he asked.

I shrugged. "I've thought a little, I guess, but right now I'm married to doing what the Lord wants me to do."

Nick nodded, but he looked down at his baby daughter instead of at me. He knew, on some level, that I was full of shit. I wanted to laugh. He and I could not have been more different. He was energized, handsome, a devout family man, politically active with several conservative groups, athletic and outgoing. He was the future of the church and everyone knew it.

But the church was up for grabs now.

"Have you been by to see Angela?" he asked.

"Not yet," I said.

Nick frowned. "I would have thought that would be your first step," he said.

"Well I, I wanted to discuss church matters with you," I stammered.

"There's a meeting scheduled," he said. "We'll be discussing 'church matters' for days and months to come. Don't you think you should be tending to your flock?"

The truth was I was scared as hell to see Angela, but how could I say that?

"I'm going by there," I said, trying not to get pissed at him. "I just wanted to drop by and discuss your thoughts on where we should go next with the church."

He sighed and patted his daughter's tiny back. "I think we should start looking for a new pastor as soon as possible," he said. "I think that's the most important thing, but, honestly—speaking of first things first, I think you should go see Angela. I think that's where you're needed."

There was nothing to do but nod and get up. "Just wanted to stop by," I said. "I was on my way over there."

He grinned. *Of course.* "We'll talk soon," he said.

"Count on it," I said, with just a little too much force behind it.

I had no choice in the matter now. I had to go see her. The funny thing is, I hadn't even realized I was avoiding talking to her, but now my hands were shaking. I went out to my car and drove over to the house of Brother Card's sister. She was a skinny blonde woman with tiny teeth and large gums, and I could tell she'd been crying when she answered the door.

"Angela's in the back there," she said.

"How is she?" I asked.

The woman pressed her fist to her lips and bit down on a sob. "She won't say nothing," she told me. "I'm glad you're here."

I gave her a hug and went back to see Angela.

She was in her cousin's room on the bed. Surprisingly, she wasn't crying. Her face was locked in a thoughtful scowl. Indifferently wearing jeans and a sweater, she just sat against the wall like someone had placed her in timeout.

"I'm so sorry," I said. I went to her and took her in my arms—'took her' being the operative words there. She lay limp against me.

Slowly she pulled away and leaned against the wall.

I patted her knee.

"Is there anything I can do?" I asked.

She examined her thumb and pressed down on a cuticle, and I noticed her freshly painted nails. I supposed she'd painted them at the sleepover, thinking of when she'd show them to me.

"The Lord loves you very much," I said. "And so do your parents. They're in heaven now, looking down on you. Do you know that? They're at peace. They're not in any pain at all."

She pressed harder, wincing a little.

"You know I'm here for you," I said, leaning in. I touched her knee. She looked at my hand like it was something she'd never seen before. "I love you very much," I told her. "You know that I'll be here for you. I love you and I always will."

I stood up and moved toward the door. There was a poster tacked to it of By His Stripes. I thought of the poster in her room peeling off the wall in flames.

"I'll come by and see you tomorrow," I said and opened the door. Then I closed it and asked, "You didn't have a diary did you?"

She shook her head. Then she frowned and asked, "Why do you want to know?"

I told her, "Well, I don't want to be at all callous right

now, but I was thinking of how bad it would be, you know, if someone found it."

She shook her head. "I don't have a diary."

"Okay. I just had to ask, you know."

She nodded almost imperceptibly.

I said, "You know, there's no reason we can't talk all the time now. Anytime at all, you know where I am."

She raised her head and looked queerly at me for a moment. Then she nodded again and went back to her thumb.

Chapter Thirteen

The meeting with the deacons went well. If a preacher is like the president of a church, the deacons are like Congress. Our deacons were mostly a bunch of old men, and they'd been serving the church for years. Now they just seemed tired. The whole meeting was run, more or less, by Nick. He'd only been a deacon for a year, but he was obviously the star of the show, everyone's bright young man. The chairman of the deacons was named E.W. Herschel. He was a retired pharmacist pushing eighty, and I don't know if he was exhausted or if he simply believed in the younger man, but he pretty much sat back chewing on his eyeglasses and let Nick control things.

After we'd prayed and sat around canonizing the Cards for an hour, Nick turned to me and said, "There's been some discussion of having you run the church in the interim." He didn't say it as if it was the greatest idea in the world.

I took a deep breath. "That's an awesome responsibility," I said.

The deacons nodded, but Nick added, "We'll need to start a pastor search after the funeral. You'd just have to handle things until we could get a new man in the pulpit."

Dr. Samuels, a retired dentist with a bald head and a booming voice, asked, "I wonder if starting the pastor search that soon won't look like we're jumping the gun a little."

Nick cocked his head to the side, "Well, Dr. Sam, I'm not disagreeing with you, but the Lord's work marches on. Seems to me that the Cards are in heaven now, and we have to carry on the Lord's work."

"I have to agree," I said. "Brother Card would certainly have put the work first."

Dr. Samuels scratched his liver spots and muttered something, but he didn't say anything else because Brother Herschel slowly sat up and slipped on his glasses. Everyone grew quiet. The chairman let Nick run the meeting, but his voice still carried more weight than anyone else's in the room. He said, "Perhaps we *should* wait a while. People need time to heal. We don't want to hamstring the new man before he's even chosen. We need time to heal as a church."

Nick shook his head. For once, things weren't really going his way. I didn't feel too much pity for him. While he was as shocked and horrified at what had happened as anyone, I don't think he'd ever really liked Card, whom he seemed to regard as a well-meaning dullard. Deep down (and he never would have *said* this) he probably saw the Cards' demise as a hard, but necessary, step in the evolution of the church. I was sure he was going to lead the pastor search, and I was sure he was going to be looking for an active administrator, a real fire-breather who was politically active and aggressive in terms of outreach. That was Nick's vision for the future—what he saw, I'm sure, as the Lord's vision. But he was going to have to wait for the old men to die off or step down before he could get some fresh blood into the pulpit. And despite what I might *say* about the need for a new preacher, I certainly wasn't going to help the pastor search along.

"While I completely agree with Nick about the need to start looking for a man to assume the leadership of the church," I said, "I also think that our primary focus in the days and weeks ahead will be to minister to the people of this church. We're all called to be ministers, not simply the pastors. I think choosing a pastor should be a top priority, to be sure. But we shouldn't hurry into anything. Brother Card's absence leaves a vacuum not easily filled, but more importantly it leaves pain and fresh wounds. It's my feeling—and I have been praying about this since I heard about the Cards—it's my feeling that we should set as our top priority the healing of this church body from this terrible event." Nick started to say something and I held up my hand to stop him. "We should be working *toward* the search for a new pastor. We should be striving toward that goal, praying on it, searching our hearts, and searching the hearts of this church body, searching for the Lord's will in this terrible time. That's the conviction of my heart."

Everyone was quiet. Nick nodded slowly—rather glumly, actually—and Brother Herschel said, "Amen to that, brother." And then that tired old man smiled, and I could tell he'd be happy if I turned out to be the pastor of the church.

I grinned politely to Nick, who was nodding and trying to repress his heartfelt objection to what I'd said. Finally he stopped nodding, and all he could muster up was, "We should pray about it."

"Indeed," Brother Herschel said and announced that we should adjourn with a word of prayer. Then he asked me, and not Nick, to say the prayer.

I smiled as I prayed. The church was mine for the taking.

Chapter Fourteen

Days passed and I heard nothing from Doolittle Norris. The papers carried the story and made a big deal of it, but they didn't say anything I didn't already know. A local minister and his wife had been brutally murdered in their home, and the home burnt to the ground, by an unknown intruder or intruders. One thing the paper did say was that investigators had determined the intruder had come in through a window in the living room because the charred remnants of the window revealed it had been left open. They'd also found a distinct—albeit mashed up—footprint on the ground nearby.

I went on about my work. I was nervous, of course, and I knew Doolittle Norris was a shaky foundation to build my future on, but I trusted him to be greedy enough to do what had to be done. After all, all I wanted was the girl; I wasn't asking for a piece of his pie. I'd made it clear I knew the stakes were higher for me than they were for him, and besides, what good would it do him to cross me? As long as he didn't find another angle, I'd be okay.

I avoided Angela as much as I could and stuck to the business at the church, going over the books, visiting the nursing home crowd and shut-ins, dropping by the hospital to see one of our teenagers who had fallen off a four-wheeler and messed up his knees. I also stayed in contact with Brother Herschel, the chairman of the deacons, and let him know, ever so subtly, that I was out there working my ass off for the church. Brother Herschel was impressed as hell and told me, "I thank the Lord for you every day, brother. I praise him for sending you here to us."

I said I was just doing what the Lord led me to do.

I even preached the Cards' funeral. That was an eye opening experience. The church was crowded and weepy, with grown men—middle-aged men in business suits—standing along the back wall, sobbing like children. I didn't even look at most of them, but the sobbing filled the sanctuary and you couldn't escape the palpable anguish, the true, ragged grief that was pouring out of people.

Did I feel guilty?

Well, let's say I felt bad. I felt bad the Cards were dead. I felt bad that people were crying, that the love of my life was crying on the front row, holding onto her brother, Gabe. He was a quiet looking guy in glasses and a dark suit. He was crying as much as she was. Everyone was crying. Hell, I cried a little, too. So, yeah, you could say I felt bad. But people were acting like the Cards were perfect, which they were not. In life, they were loved by some, tolerated by some, and loathed by the rest. It's not as if Higher Living Baptist Church had been a fucking playground before the Cards died. There'd been a fair share of backstabbing and gossip and bitching and moaning. Sister Card had pissed people off. Brother Card had pissed people off. It wasn't all hugs and kisses.

I preached a nice service, though. It was my first funeral, of course, but I did, I thought, a superlative job. I talked about God's will, and the mystery of suffering, the presence of evil in the world, and the plan of salvation. I talked about Sister Card's cooking and her dedication to her husband's ministry. I talked about Angela and how she was dear to all of us in the church, how God was looking out for her, how he had a wonderful plan for her life. I trumpeted Brother Card's faithfulness, and his vision for the church, and all he had done in the service of the Lord.

It was a hell of a talking I gave them that day.

But the whole time I was thinking, *why can't they see what a bunch of bullshit this is?*

The Cards were dead, deader than Bonnie and Clyde. Someone had murdered them. Had it really been God's plan? That day, I told the weeping congregation that everything was in God's hands, and evil and hatred and loss and suffering would all be wiped away in the blink of an eye when Christ returned. But the whole time I wondered: do they really believe this? They seemed to. They cried and held onto each other and stared up at the cross on the wall behind me and nodded their heads. They seemed to feel comforted.

Maybe that's all that counts to people. If there wasn't suffering, men would feel no need to believe in God. The sick part is, if there is a God, he must have planned it that way.

After the graveside service, I ran into the chairman of deacons and Nick. They were standing by the cars, hands in their pockets, staring at the grass.

Brother E.W. Herschel had the face of a Confederate general. He was a creased-skinned old man with deep eye sockets and a stern mouth that was always pulling back into a grimace. Thick bifocals rested on a heavy nose full of gray hair, and his sideburns extended down to his jowls. He shook my hand and held it. "Powerful sermon, brother. Very fitting."

Nick nodded his assent.

"I was honored to do it," I exclaimed. "My first funeral to

preach. I never thought it would be under these conditions. I appreciate your support, your example."

The old man patted my hand.

Nick said, "The Lord gives us what we need, I guess."

I let go of Brother Herschel's hand and said, "Absolutely."

Brother Herschel told me, "I think we've all been pleased to see how hard you've been working these past days. Incredibly difficult. Incredibly trying circumstances to find yourself thrust into leadership."

Nick looked at the grass some more.

I told Brother Herschel, "We can only do what we can. We can only supplicate ourselves to the Lord and allow the Holy Ghost to work through us." And on and on. You see how it went.

Nick couldn't take much more. "I need to go say a few words to Gabe and Angela," he said. "I'll talk to you all later."

"Take care," I said.

He walked off.

"That's a fine man," I told Brother Herschel.

"Mm," he said. "He is. He's young."

"Older than me," I said.

"Mm. But you're an old soul. Nick's as fine a man as we have in the church. I was the one that nominated him for his deaconship, did you know that?"

"I didn't," I lied.

"Mm. I did. And he hasn't let me down. Not by a long ways. But he's young, always in a hurry. Being in a hurry is a characteristic of the young, I reckon."

"I reckon it is."

"I don't see that in you, though."

I said something about wanting to go at the Lord's speed, whatever that speed may be.

Brother Herschel was wearing a red flower in the lapel of his dark suit coat, and he took it out and rubbed its stem between his thumb and forefinger. "Men in a hurry change the world. But the world they change has to be run by men with a steady hand on the wheel. Would you agree with that?"

"Yes, sir."

"Mm. Like players in a symphony. Everybody playing his part, all led by a conductor. You're a man with a steady hand."

"I hope so. That's my true hope."

He put his flower back in his lapel and patted me on the shoulder. "You keep up the good work, brother. You just keep it up."

As he walked off, I smiled and thought, *Any day now. Any day now.*

It took about three weeks. I kept my nose to the grindstone in the interim. I preached both the morning and night services on Sunday and combined the youth and adult service on Wednesday night in the guise of "Letting the kids know we're all still a family." The Wednesday night service in particular was a smashing success because it let the adults feel that they were involved with the youth. I arranged a mission trip down to Mexico for the following year, kept up my visitation at the hospitals and nursing homes and made the rounds on Monday night visitations, which involved me and Nick going to the homes of a bunch of deadbeats and backsliders and trying to get them to come to church.

One Monday night, after we'd wasted an hour in a trailer with a shirtless man who swilled beer and stared numbly at us while we read him Bible verses, Nick and I rode back to the church in his car.

"That went well," I muttered.

Nick shrugged. "We planted some seeds, anyway."

"He was watering them with beer," I said.

Nick grinned curiously as he kept his eyes on the road. "You have a unique sense of humor sometimes," he said. Nick was the sort of man for whom the word *unique* was always an insult.

"I suppose it's my way of dealing with grim circumstances," I said.

"I suppose," he said.

That fucking drunk back there didn't give two shits about the plan of salvation, I wanted to say. I didn't say anything, of course, and just sat there.

Nick finally blurted out, "I was thinking about the pastor search committee. I think we should start looking soon. How would you feel about that?"

"The sooner the better," I said. I saw no point in telling him something he didn't want to hear.

"Really? I thought you might be opposed to the idea."

"Why would I be opposed to it?"

"Oh," Nick said. "I don't know. It seemed to me as if you had your eye on the job. I don't mean that in a bad way. I just thought you had your eye on the job."

"I don't see why. I've never expressed anything along those lines."

"Are you saying you don't want the job?"

"Nick, my philosophy is to stay open to the Holy Spirit. I certainly wouldn't rule out looking for a new pastor. I wouldn't rule out taking the job if the church wanted me to. I wouldn't rule anything out. It's about God's will, not mine."

"Well, I certainly agree with that, but—"

"Good."

"—I'm just looking at the situation and trying to get a

feel for what you have in mind. I'd like to proceed in as organized a way as possible."

"I've tried to be clear about what I'm thinking. I think we should bend ourselves to the will of the Lord. If you feel his prodding, if the deacons feel his prodding, and if the church seems ready for it, then I say the sooner the better."

Nick said, "I don't feel like you've answered my question."

"What is your question?"

"What do you want?"

"The will of God."

Nick took a deep breath.

"I'm sorry if that exasperates you, Nick," I said. "But honestly, I'm trying to keep all options open. I'm not sure why you're having a hard time accepting that."

"I feel as if your actions are giving me a different answer than your mouth."

"I'm sorry you feel that way. It really grieves me that you feel that way, and I don't know what I've done to deserve that. I've just tried to do my job the best I could. Really. Honestly. Outside of doing my job as well as I can, I don't know what my 'actions' have been."

I had him there. Nick couldn't name what I'd done wrong because I hadn't done anything wrong.

He took another deep breath. "Look, maybe that was out of line. I don't mean to act as if I don't appreciate the work you've done, just…I think you're skimping on your true ambitions. I just want to know what you want."

"I say, the Lord's will be done."

Nick swallowed a mouthful of disbelief and forced out a smile. He didn't say another word the rest of the way.

•   •   •

A week later, it was done. At a meeting of the deacons, Brother Herschel announced, "Brother Webb, we've decided we'd like you to take over as pastor of Higher Living Baptist Church."

The deacons beamed at me, smiling and nodding. Nick stared at his hands.

"Is this the unanimous decision of the deacons?" I asked.

"No," Nick said.

The room stopped and his face turned red from embarrassment. The chairman's mouth hung open a little.

Doctor Samuels took off his glasses and rubbed the bridge of his nose. "Is that called for, Nick?" he asked. "Shouldn't we be speaking as one, speaking to this church and to this city with one voice?"

Nick took a deep breath and said, "Brothers, I apologize for that outburst. It was childish." Then he stood up and turned to me and said, "I can only tell you, however, what God has laid on my heart. I've been on my knees about this every day since Brother Card died, and I've been reduced to tears about it." He looked hard at me now, trying to be as calm as possible, but I could see his revulsion for me in his stupid, handsome face. "I don't think you are the man for this job. I don't think the Lord wants you as pastor of this church. And I don't think I'm alone in this. There are others in this room who feel the same way but don't want to say anything." He hung his head. "I don't have any hate in my heart, brothers. Please believe me. But I can't go against what I know in my heart is right."

With that he turned and walked out of the room.

For a while we all sat in silence. I waited. Brother Herschel shook his head and closed his eyes. The minister of music, a chubby guy whose sole ambition in life was to do as little work as possible, sat there with his mouth open. Dr. Samuels looked ready to cry. I waited, and when the moment was just right, I said, "Let's pray."

I prayed a good one that day. I prayed for strength and guidance, prayed for all of us and for Nick and for God's mercy and for a spirit of Christian love. I prayed that the church would rise up as an eagle, that we would all know we were in the hands of the Lord. But I was cussing on the inside. I knew Nick could split the church if he wanted, and I knew that the negative publicity wouldn't do me any good. I also knew that the news of his walking out the room would be shot around town in seconds after that meeting was adjourned. So I prayed a long time because I knew things weren't going to work out exactly like I'd planned.

Chapter Fifteen

And then it all started to fall apart.

The first blow came when I reached the house. After the meeting at church, I'd driven around for a while just thinking. Driving around didn't do much good, though, and I was still feeling tired and stressed when I walked through the front door. I didn't have both feet inside when the phone started ringing. I sighed. I wanted to turn around and leave, but I had to answer it.

It was her.

"I want to see you," she snapped.

"Maybe tomorrow we—"

"Now," she said. "At the elementary by my aunt's house."

Then she hung up.

I cradled the receiver and leaned against the wall. I just stood there getting my senses together for a second before I headed back out the door.

It was a ten minute drive over to the school, and when I pulled up she was there already, standing on the concrete steps leading up to the front door. School was out and the parking lot was empty, and it felt as if we were meeting in a ghost town. As I got out of my car, a bitter gust of wind blew a Wal-Mart bag across the asphalt like suburban sage brush. Angela wore a nondescript yellow sweater and blue jeans, and she stood there in the cold like she was a goddamn cop.

As soon as I got out of my car, she rushed down the steps.
"What's wrong?" I asked.
"Are you going to run the church?" she demanded.
"What?"
"Are you?"
"Well, I—I don't know really," I stammered. "There's been some talk."
"Just answer me," she said. She put her hand on the hood of my car as if to steady herself and sort of bent over like she might be sick.
"Are you all right?" I asked. I looked around at the vacant parking lot and the empty playground.
Squeezing her eyes shut, she said, "Just answer my question!"
"I told you I don't know, Angela," I said.
She stood up straight and looked me in the eye. "You're always talking," she said, "but you never say anything. You know whether or not you're going to be the pastor. You're not stupid. Why won't you just tell me what you know?"
"Look," I snapped. "I don't know. But I think so, yes. So if you just want a one word answer—if that's your idea of 'talking'—then the one word answer is yes. Are you happy now?"
She shook her head and leaned against the car. When I drifted toward her, she put her hand out to stop me.
"Just... Don't touch me. Not right now."
"Would you tell me what's wrong then?"
She took a deep breath. "It's my father's church. You can't just take it away from him. It's not right."
"Baby," I said, "you're talking irrationally."
"I don't want you to take it away from him."
"No one is taking it away from him," I said softly. "He died. I am so, so, so sorry he died, but he did. What do you

want to happen? Do you want the church to have no leader? Think about it. I know you're upset, but the church needs a leader. If they want me to be that leader, don't you think I should do it?"

She stared across the parking lot and the wind blew again, stirring the creaky swings on the playground.

She looked back at me finally and sucked on her bottom lip. She was just a kid, but I could tell there was something turning inside of her.

"Where were you the night my parents… Where were you?"

My stomach felt terrible and heavy, like it was full of hot water. "Angela…I was home."

She shook her head and started to cry.

"Baby…"

"I called there," she said.

"I didn't answer," I said. "I don't answer the phone every time it rings, you know."

She wiped the tears away with the white knuckles of her fist. "You're not telling me the truth."

"Of course I am. You're talking crazy. I don't always answer the phone. I sat out on the porch and read a little. I… ate. I watched some television. I was there all night.

"Look," I said, "I don't want your father's church. The deacons asked me to fill the pastor position for a while and I said I would. But if you don't want me to, I won't. If you have some bizarre notion that I'm after the church, I just won't take the position of pastor, that's all. There's nothing I want in this world but to be with you. You know that."

A car turned down the street and I tensed up. Angela was obviously crying. What could I do but stand there and let her cry? The car slowed down as it neared the school, and I kept my back to it. Then it turned into the school's driveway.

It pulled up alongside us, and Gabe got out and said, "Hello" to me and looked at his sister. She stared at the ground.

I extended my hand, and Gabe gave me a weak handshake. He was wearing gloves and a heavy coat, but he looked like he might be shivering. To her he said, "Been looking all over for you, Buttons."

"Sorry," she said.

"It's okay," he told her. "Maybe we should get on back to Aunt Carol's."

Still staring at me, she said, "Okay."

I scrambled to think of what to say. I'm always the talker. Saying nothing was like putting on an orange prison jumpsuit. But I couldn't think of one goddamn word. I waited on her.

"Let's go," she said to her brother.

I didn't think she was going to say anything to me—which would be suspicious—so I blurted out, "I hope you get to feeling better." It was stupid, but my mind had ground to a halt.

Walking past me she said, "Thanks for talking to me, Brother Geoffrey. I really appreciate it."

Her brother watched her go to the car, and then he looked at me. I'd never noticed before how much Gabe resembled his father.

"Thanks," he said, but he didn't mean it. In the way he said it, he resembled his mother.

I fumbled out something about wanting to be a help in a difficult time, but he ignored me and went to the car, got in and pulled out of the drive.

• • •

I went home and for the next few hours I just sat on the couch and stared at the walls.

And I thought. I thought about the Cards, about Doolittle Norris, about Nick and the deacons; and I thought about Angela. I had no idea what was going on inside her head. Why would she think I had something to do with the death of her parents? It may sound odd, but the idea made me mad. What had I ever done to give her any reason to suspect me?

And then it hit me. Maybe the problem was me. Maybe I wasn't as hidden and smart as I thought I was. Maybe the problem had been me all along.

But I pushed that aside. Why think negative thoughts, right?

But then it occurred to me that if there was a god, then maybe he was punishing me.

No, I thought. That can't be. Too many people get away with too many different kinds of things. What I had done was wrong, I could grant that, but I wasn't the worst man in the world. Why should I be punished for my sins if so many had escaped punishment?

I fell to sleep with that thought. I would not be punished.

An hour or so later, the pointed toe of a cowboy boot nudged me awake. It poked my shoulder like the tip of a spear.

"Hey," a deep voice said.

It took me a few seconds to focus, but when I looked up, Doolittle Norris was standing over me.

Chapter Sixteen

"Get up," he said.

He was standing, big and bowlegged, by my head. I eased into a sitting position and rubbed my temples. My head ached a little like I'd been drinking.

"What are you doing here?" I muttered.

He wore an open jean jacket with wool lining, and his thumbs were hitched on his belt loops. A big smile shoved his scarlet cheeks back up to his ears as he said, "Get your coat and meet me behind the 7-11 over by the church, buddy boy. We need to talk."

"About what?"

"About your case. There's been a development."

"Why don't we talk here?"

He shook his head affably. "Naw, I don't like it here. Every second I'm in this house I take one step closer to the penitentiary. Get up and meet me there in five minutes. We'll go somewhere where the whole damn town ain't watching."

He left. I slipped into my shoes, grabbed my coat and went outside. The night was blisteringly cold and my car wouldn't have time to heat up by the time I got to the 7-11, so I didn't even turn it on. My mind was a blank as I drove. I felt as though I was being pulled along, pulled into whatever it was that life finally had in store for me. I wasn't even frightened. If anything, I was impatient.

The Sheriff sat parked around back by a dumpster. I got out, crossed the little parking lot strewn with candy wrappers and plastic bottles, and climbed into his truck.

"Fucking cold," he said.

I said it was, and he turned up the heater. Another of his books on tape was talking, and he didn't touch the radio. Neither of us said anything as the book on tape, a biography of Charles Lindbergh, told us about his transatlantic flight.

Norris pulled out of the parking lot, and I had no idea anymore where we were going. Out beyond the edge of the trees, I saw distant rows of lighted homes, warm and orderly little lights getting farther away as we slipped into the dark. When we pulled off of the dirt road and onto the highway I realized we were leaving Little Rock.

I wanted to ask where we were going, but before I could say anything, Norris switched off the radio and began talking about Lindbergh. "Guy had to have balls to take out across the fucking ocean in a little lightweight plane back in '27," he said. For the next twenty or thirty minutes, all he talked about was Charles Lindbergh.

He talked about the flight, flying conditions back in the twenties, the kidnapping of the baby, the subsequent trial, the unfortunate flirtation with the Nazis in the thirties. The entire time he was talking we were heading north from Little Rock, towards the mountains.

"Where are we going?" I asked finally.

He seemed irritated I'd interrupted his recounting of the life of Lindbergh, and he shrugged, "We're leaving town. Getting far enough away to clear our heads and have a serious conversation."

We passed a diesel. "Let's have it now," I said.

He just shrugged again. "You can wait, Mr. Preacher."

"No. I can't," I said. "I want to talk now."

He didn't say anything. We passed some cars.

"Now, goddamn it!" I shouted.

Norris shifted in his seat, taking the wheel firmly in his left hand and adjusting the rearview mirror with his right hand. Then, after he'd checked to make sure there were no cars directly behind us, he clenched a fist and backhanded me. The truck lurched a little, and Norris realigned it neatly.

Shock spread over my face like a cracking windshield. Warm blood ran down my lips.

"Lean back and pinch your nose," he said, wiping his hand on the sleeve of my coat. "Hurt?"

I leaned back and pinched my nose and didn't answer. My face felt like it was growing.

"You hurt?" he asked again, friendly and folksy.

"Yes," I said.

"I bet."

My eyes filled with tears, and I could taste the snot and blood in the back of my throat.

"You still want to talk?" he said.

I shook my head.

"Good."

We drove in silence for a few miles before he laughed. "Funny thing is, now I want to talk," he said.

"Don't let me stop you," I said.

He chuckled. "I've nursed a lot of bleeding noses in my day, you know."

"I imagine."

"My brothers and me fought all the time, beating the shit out of each other. And my old man...my old man handed out bloody noses like they were Easter candy. Miserable son of a bitch, that guy. Mean bastard."

"My father was abusive, too," I said, hoping to make a connection.

Doolittle Norris just laughed. He laughed as if I'd said something hilarious. "You recovered triumphantly," he said. "A real credit to the human spirit."

He leaned over, grinning at me. "Hey," he said, "can you keep a secret?"

I actually almost laughed at that. "All I have is secrets," I said.

"Brother, you can say that again. I never met a guy with more fucking secrets than you. And coming from me, that's saying something."

"What's the secret you want me to keep?" I asked.

"There's a little spot on the side of a mountain up here where my grandfather once had a still. He was a shiner. His father had been a shiner, too. Sold shine to the Union troops when they came through."

"Quite the family tradition," I gargled out. "That's the big secret?"

"Well," he said, "there are bodies buried up there."

"Yeah?"

"Sure, my old man stuck some in the ground up there. In fact, he's buried up there himself. Been out there for thirty-plus years." Doolittle thought about that for a little bit. Then he said, "The Thanksgiving my mother was pregnant with Lacey, the old man got drunk. Spent the whole day sitting in the living room sipping homemade rotgut whiskey and muttering to himself. We tiptoed around him, but sometimes he'd glare up at you so hard it'd make your balls hurt. The old man was just plain scary. He didn't eat with us when my mother called us to the table. He just sat out there in the living room grumbling into his whiskey while we ate in silence. Well by nine o'clock, he was completely soused, and he gets up and stumbles into the kitchen. My mother was washing up our dishes and the old man suddenly started demanding

Thanksgiving dinner. I don't know what she said, but she was never, ever—not for one day in her life—was my mother ever the docile type. So she smarted off or something—told him to get his own goddamn turkey. And he grabbed her by the hair, yanked her head back like he was tearing the lid off something, and he punched her. Now we'd seen him slap the shit out of her before, and even though she was a little woman, she always gave as good as she got. But that night he fucking punched her, fat and pregnant with his baby, he punched her like you'd punch a man, and she hit the floor like she wasn't going to get back up. 'What do you have to say to me now?' That's what he said. She was sprawled at his feet, nose broke and bloody, and he says, 'What do you have to say to me now?' And my mother—this tiny little woman—she climbs up, hoists herself up by the edge of the sink, reaches her hand into the soapy dishes and before he had a chance to know what the hell was going on, she stuck a fucking carving fork in his heart.

"I'll never forget that. The blood on his shirt was soapy. Momma just stood there looking down at him. She's only about five foot tall, but, Jesus, she seemed like a fucking mountain to me at that moment. Just stood there looking down at him. Then she looks at me and my brothers and sisters. And you know what? She wasn't scared. Not one damn bit. She looked at us, and her eyes were wild and hard, and for a second, I got to tell you, I thought she was going to kill us all. My older brother Van started crying. He was always a little weak-kneed. She looked at him for a second, and then she pointed at me and said, 'You go fetch the shovel.' She was like a general.

"That night me and Van helped her bury him out there in the freezing cold. Mostly me. I wasn't no older than my son is now, but Van was still crying, and I was always pretty clear headed. That was that. The old man's been out there rotting in the dirt for thirty years."

"Why are you telling me this?"

Doolittle didn't hear me. He was thinking about things, I suppose, thinking about his father's murder that frigid Thanksgiving night. It didn't seem like he'd ever given it much thought. Finally, he shook his head, and, as if to put the period at the end of a sentence, he just sighed, "A woman is a hell of a thing."

It was amazing how little he was aware of me, like I was a bag of garbage he was hauling to the dump.

"May I ask a question?"

He grinned and reached for his spit cup. "Go ahead."

"You said you wanted to talk about the case. Would you mind telling me what's going on with the investigation?"

"Not as easy as you think, keeping the heat off of you. I can pull strings with the best of them, but I actually have people working for me who know how to investigate murders." He spit. "But that ain't what I wanted to talk to you about."

"What did you want to talk about, then?"

He sighed. "Well, I found that envelope. Went by your house last night and picked it up. I guess you've been too involved with your church work to think about that kind of stuff very much."

Goddamn it.

That's all I could think: God. Damn. It.

"At my house," I said.

"Mm." He shook his head. "Leaving it there was stupid, you know."

I nodded. "It was a bluff. But I figured it was too…" I choked a little, rolled down the window and spat a glob of blood. I rolled the window back up and said, "Too obvious."

"Yeah," he said, almost kindly. We were like two opposing coaches discussing a football game I'd lost. "I can see that."

"So you don't need me anymore."

"Oh man, we're way beyond me not needing you. You're a time bomb. You killed the preacher and his wife." He shook his head. Then he chuckled. "Christ. I didn't see that coming. I'll give you that one. You surprised me by killing the Cards."

"It was an accident."

"Yeah."

I leaned forward.

"And now you have everything you want," I said.

"Pretty much," he replied. "I got plans, though. Once the money starts coming in from the aluminum plant, who knows where it could all lead?"

I put my hand on the buckle of my seat belt. "Where do you want it to lead?"

"Honestly?" he said cheerfully. "I'm thinking state senate."

I put my head back, but I tried to nod. "Is that a real possibility?" As gently as I could, I pressed the button on my seat belt. Norris shifted his weight onto his left hip. His coat fell open and out of the corner of my eye I glanced the gun on his hip.

"You bet," Norris answered. He took the steering wheel in his left hand.

"Ambitious."

"Well," he said, casually inching his right hand down to his gun, "way I see it, ambition is just a dream with a hard-on."

I laughed, and he laughed too, and I flung myself at him and jerked the wheel hard to the right. We careened into the side of an eighteen-wheeler and the passenger's side window shattered and sprayed glass across us. Norris growled and cursed "Goddamn you" and elbowed me in the head. But he didn't take his foot off the petal; he had it pressed to the floor for leverage against me as he hammered my face and neck. But I wasn't fighting him; I was fighting the wheel. I gave it another hard jerk and we went into a spin.

Then I was tumbling. It was like I was caught in a tornado; sight and sound and sensation had broken apart and swirled together. The dashboard lights and the windshield, the explosion of glass and the scream of metal across pavement. Norris's yelling and my yelling. We slammed into each other, just two objects in the torrent, two hands clapped together and thrown apart. The truck flipped again, and then I was in flight outside the truck. The weight of air and gravity pulled at me, and then the earth smashed into me, and I was on my side and skidding down the grassy median while things were dropping and breaking all around. Cars were stopping.

And then there was silence and frosty grass and sky.

And after that, there was nothing for a while.

Chapter Seventeen

I woke up in a hospital bed. A black woman in orange scrubs was leaning over me and adjusting something above my head. Behind her on a beige wall hung a Monet print, and above that hung a television. The sound wasn't on.

"Looks like you're waking up," the woman said.

I tried to nod, but my neck was in a brace.

"Jesus," I said. "Am I paralyzed?"

"No."

"Just tell me if I am."

She shrugged. Her skin was caramel-colored and smelled like fresh lotion. "Okay, I will. If you ever get paralyzed, I'll tell you. But you're not paralyzed. Which is amazing. You got some cuts and some strained muscles and some broke fingers, but the rest of you is okay. You ain't feeling much because we have you doped up."

"Thank the Lord," I said. It just popped out of my mouth, so maybe I meant it. On the television, a fat guy dressed like Cupid was selling cars.

The nurse smiled and turned to mess with something on a cart by the bed. "You best thank somebody," she said, "because there isn't a logical reason why you're still alive and relatively…"

"Unscathed?"

She said, "You're a lucky man."

"This is the first time," I said.

"Well, you picked a good time to start."

I thought about Norris. "What about the other man in the truck?"

She shook her head and patted my bare shoulder. Her hand was smooth and warm. "I don't know about your friend," she said. "They're still working on him, but he's in pretty bad shape. He was in the middle of half a ton of broken metal and glass. But they're still working on him. We got some good doctors here."

"Where am...am I?"

"You're at Connor County Hospital."

My head felt thick and spongy. "In Stock's Settlement. Pretty far...north. North. Why did they bring me, us...me here?"

"You're so full of questions," she said. Then she held up something that looked like a tube of lipstick attached to a wire. "If you wake up and you need me there's a little button and you can buzz me."

"Lipstick. Can't..." I drifted off for a second. "What—"

"You're going to sleep now," she said. "Medication. You'll feel—"

I assume she said I'd feel fine.

And I did.

The next time I awoke there was a balloon in the room. It was floating in the corner and read: GET WELL SOON!! in red letters. The air from the ceiling vent stirred it and it thumped against the wall. On the television, a man in a blue shirt and tie pointed at a map of Arkansas while computerized snowflakes blinked over the Ozarks.

I lay there a while watching the weather man pointing

at the weather. Then the door opened and people entered. I couldn't really turn my head to see them, though, so I moaned out, "Hello?"

A middle-aged woman walked up. With her little teeth and her big gums she looked familiar, but I couldn't place her at first. She looked to the other side of the room and said, "Well, c'mon. He's awake. Don't be bashful."

Then it hit me. Brother Card's sister. Angela's aunt.

"Angela?" I said.

Her aunt smiled, and then said again to the other side of the room, "Don't be bashful, now."

Angela walked to the edge of the bed. A black turtleneck sweater choked her pale face, and she just stared down at me.

"Are you okay?" she asked.

"I think so. I just woke up. I'm a little dazed."

"Yeah," she said.

She pulled at the hem of her sweater.

Ms. Card said, "She had to come see you, Brother Webb. She was real concerned when she heard about your accident. Everybody was."

"I appreciate that," I said. I looked at Ms. Card. "Thank you for the balloon."

"Oh, that was from folks at the church," she said. "A lot of people have been up here in the last day or so. We're just the lucky ones that got you when you was waking up."

"Do you know anything about…Doolittle?" I asked.

Angela grimaced. I could tell she was chewing on the inside of her cheek, and I wanted to tell her to stop, but I couldn't, of course. I couldn't be that familiar with her in front of her aunt.

Ms. Card told me, "He's still upstairs. He's…it's a rough time for him right now. Nick and Lacey are up there."

For some reason, that sent chills crawling across me like an army of ants. "Nick is here?"

"Sure. He's been in to see you, I think."

"He has," Angela said.

"Everybody's concerned," Ms. Card said. "The kids from your youth group are all real concerned. Aren't they, Angela?"

"Yes," Angela said.

"And after what happened to…" Ms. Card shook her head. "That church has been through a lot." She put her arm around Angela. "So you stay healthy, Brother Webb. Those kids need you."

"I will," I said.

Angela glanced at the door like she was afraid it would disappear.

"How are you?" I asked her.

"Fine."

"She's just bashful," Ms. Card said. "All she talked about was getting up here to see you and now she's here she's quiet as a mouse." She rubbed Angela's shoulder and told her, "But you've been through a lot lately, so it's okay to be quiet."

"Absolutely," I said. My head felt thick.

Angela started chewing her bottom lip and nodded. "I think we should go."

"Well, he ain't been awake five minutes, sweetie."

"He looks tired."

Ms. Card looked down at me. "You do," she said.

I nodded. "I might want to get some more sleep," I said. "I sort of feel myself drifting, so I may not have any choice."

Ms. Card patted my arm. "You get some more sleep. You'll be out of here soon. You just remember everybody is praying for you."

"Thank you," I said.

Angela, still biting her lip, didn't look at me. "We'll see you later," she said.

"Thank you for coming, Angela," I said. "I really appreciate it."

She said, "Okay" and started for the door.

Ms. Card patted my arm, blessed me and they left.

I stared at a blank spot on the wall. I wanted to cry.

Then Angela rushed back into the room. She stopped at the side of my bed.

"Are we alone?" I asked her.

"Yes. I only have a second, though," she said.

"Don't be scared."

"Okay."

"I'm going to be okay."

She stared at me and chewed her cheek. "Everyone wants to know why you were in the truck with Sheriff Norris."

"We were talking about his son Tim."

"Why?"

"What do you mean? I'm the youth minister. Tim is one of the kids in my youth group."

She stared at my face like she was trying to decide what it was made of.

"Oh," she said.

"And I was asking him about the case involving your parents."

"What'd he say?"

"Nothing really. Said he couldn't really discuss an ongoing investigation."

She stared at me a little more and tapped her fingers on the bed rail. "Oh." She looked back over her shoulder. "I have to go."

"Yeah. I guess so." I touched her hand. "I miss you, baby."

She said, "Okay" and turned and left, but before she got

to the door, she swung around and came back and bent down and kissed me roughly on the lips. Then she was gone. I heard the door glide shut.

For a while, I lay there listening to the silence. I thought of Norris fighting for his life upstairs. I thought about the eventual talk I was going to have to have with Nick. I thought about having to talk to the cops.

When I fell asleep I thought I knew the worst of it.

Chapter Eighteen

Sometime later I awoke. Night darkened my window. I rustled, blinked, and coughed a few times. "He's awake," a deep voice said. The voice didn't seem happy.

A young man I didn't know was sitting in the chair by my bed. Bald, with a horn-shaped goatee that curved down and jabbed his clavicle, he was muscular to the point of grotesqueness. When he stood up, the wall behind him vanished. In a voice at the lower end of the human register, he said, "I'm going to get Grandmom."

From somewhere behind him, another man muttered, "Okay" and the muscular young man strode out. Then the other man walked over to my bed and used the electronic doodad to elevate my head. This hurt just about everything and I let out a moan. The drugs were gone, and my body ached.

The man was short with intense dark eyes and curly hair the color of steel wool. He was wearing a pressed white shirt with a gray tie and looked, to me, like a lawyer.

He asked, "Do you know where you are?"

"Connor County Hospital," I said.

"That's correct," he said. He rested his hands on my guard rail. His hands were clean and smelled pleasantly of aftershave.

"What time is it?" I asked.

"It's about seven."

"At night?"

"Yes. You've been asleep for the better part of two days."

I nodded. My head was still in a brace, and still hurt, but it didn't hurt as much as I would have thought. I ached all over, like I'd taken a beating, but I could tell—could just feel—that I was okay. I've always had that kind of luck, the kind of luck that ensures that you're always healthy enough to fall deeper into trouble. I'll never die accidentally.

"Do you know who I am?" he asked.

"No," I said.

"Vandover Norris. Friends call me Van."

"I've heard of you. You're a lawyer."

"Yes, I am."

"And Sheriff Norris's brother."

"Yes."

"I see. How is he?"

"He's dead."

Under my clean, warm sheets I felt my skin turn to ice. "I'm sorry," I said.

He shrugged and looked over his shoulder.

The muscular young man had returned pushing a little old woman in a wheel chair.

Her pinched face was powdered white, and a thick gob of lipstick sat on her tiny, toothless mouth like a drop of blood on a corpse. When the young man stopped, the old woman rose slowly from the chair. A long, snowy ponytail hung over her yellow flower print dress, and she brushed it back.

When she spoke, her broken voice was soft, even fragile, but her gray eyes were as dead as gravel. "Are you…the one…who killed my son?" she asked.

I could not think of how to answer her. Next to me, Van Norris seemed to shrink.

The tiny old lady stared at me. As she began to speak, her voice quivered, unsure from syllable to syllable, but not from anything resembling fear. Her eyes sparked to life, like coal catching fire, yet they were still trapped in a body that was wasting away beneath her. "I asked you...a question. Did you kill...my son?"

"No ma'am."

"No ma'am," she sighed. With the young man standing behind her like a wall, she leaned across the guard rail, close enough that I could smell her lipstick. "I know...all about you," she said. Her voice was thin and frayed, but the closer she got the more her powdered skeleton seemed as hard as a corkscrew. "You're a ...degenerate, a murderer, a molester of little girls..." She turned to her son. "What do you...call that, Van? A man who...molests little girls?"

"A pedophile."

She turned back to me. "That's right. A pedophile. That's...what you are."

I shook my head. "No ma'am," I said. "She's a little young but she not..."

She patted my arm again like she was my grandmother. "I want you...to be quiet now," she said. "Like a little baby... like a little baby in a crib. Quiet...as can be."

I nodded.

"Ian," she said, "give me...my purse, dear."

The young man handed her a wide maroon handbag. She lay it on my bed and unsnapped the silver clasp in the middle and took out a small handgun. Like it was a pet, she scooped it up with both hands and held it out to me as if she wanted me to take it. I didn't move and neither did anyone else. She was simply showing it to me. Then, holding the barrel with one hand she tried to pull the hammer back with her other hand.

"Tough," she said. "I don't know why … they make these things…so hard to use. Hope I never get…jumped in the alley." She pulled on the gun some more and shook her head. She said, "Ian, honey…"

The young man reached around, took the gun, cocked the hammer back and put it back in her hands.

"Thank you," she said. She put the gun against my sternum, Van said, "Mother," and she pulled the trigger.

And nothing. Just a sharp metallic click.

"Weepin' Jesus," she said. She looked at the gun as if it were a phaser from Star Trek.

Pain shot up my neck and tears formed in my eyes.

"Did I do something wrong?" she asked.

Ian cocked the gun once more, she pointed it at me and pulled the trigger, and it clicked again. Ian took the gun, sprang the magazine and said, "No bullets, Grandmom."

"Well for…Christ's sake."

"You forgot to load it," he said. His voice had as much personality as a sheet of ice.

Van wiped his face, and I could hear his sweat hit the floor. "Mother, we're in the middle of a hospital," he pleaded.

"I told you…I should keep it…loaded," the old woman told Ian.

"You don't need a loaded gun around the house," he replied.

"I would have…swore I loaded it…'fore we come up here."

"Jesus," Van said.

"You leave it on the counter?" Ian asked.

"I reckon I did. I bet you…I left the…loaded thing, the, what do you call it…"

"Magazine," Ian said.

"I left it…on the counter."

"Can we get down to business?" Van said sharply.

His mother looked at him as if he were a fool. "What's it...look like...I was doing?"

"Mother. Not here. Not now. For Christ's— We can't..." He rubbed his face and then he looked at Ian. "You knew she was bringing a gun. You let her bring a gun into the hospital."

The young man replied, "I don't tell her what to do, Van. No one tells her what to do."

"But it seemed like a good idea to you, bringing a fucking gun into the hospital?"

"She doesn't run ideas past me, Van. Or you. Or anybody else. I'm not sure why you seem to have forgotten that."

I wasn't making a sound, but I was trying to find the button for the nurse. I was trying to find it without looking for it, but when I did glance down I saw that the old lady was holding it. She smiled at me and dropped it over the side of the bed out of my reach.

"That's enough," she said. She held out her arm—and the young man took it in his huge paws like she was made of crystal—and helped her into her chair. "Now," she said, settling in. "What are we...going to do here?"

I said, "I don't—"

"Shh," she soothed. "I'm...talking to Van, now. You just... be quiet and listen."

Van folded his arms across his chest. "What would you like done? That's really the question."

"Well," she said, pointing a knotty finger at me. "First thing is...we need this...young feller dead...and in the ground before...tomorrow morning."

Van sighed.

"What?" she said.

"Nothing. It'll just be a little more complicated than you think."

She slapped her knee. For the first time, she sounded irritated. Her voice was as tough as hickory when she said, "Jesus Christ in Heaven! It's always about 'difficult' with you."

Van's shoulders stooped.

She stared at him. "I ain't got…Doolittle around no more," she said in cracking voice. It seemed like she might cry. "That means…I need you to be a man…Can't you just…be a man? Can't you just please… for once…try to be a man… and do for me…what needs to be done?"

He rubbed the bridge of his nose. "Of course," he said. "But hear me out: the wreck was on the news. This man was in the truck with the sheriff when he died. People are asking questions. Reporters are poking around. Doolittle was already a controversy all by himself. Now he's died under questionable circumstances, and not only that, but when he died, he was with this man—a man who is already vaguely linked to a double murder. It has all the makings of a big story. There are guys down at the papers and news stations who live on this type of thing. They breathe it like air. They're already asking why Doolittle and this guy were heading north. They're already asking why he hasn't been taken down to Little Rock. They're already asking if it has anything to do with the murder of that preacher and his wife. None of it is getting into print yet, but all the right people are asking all the right questions. I'm not saying it can't be done." Van rubbed his face. "But I am strongly urging caution right now."

Mrs. Norris said, "Ian?"

The giant behind her said, "Yes, Grandmom."

"I want you…to remember this day…the day your uncle… showed his true colors. You know what his number one… true color is?"

"No, Grandmom."

"Yellow," she said. She pointed at me and told Van, very sweetly, in a voice completely even and strong, "You have to get rid of him, dear. I'm sure you can see that. I mean, we're sitting here discussing it in front of him, aren't we?"

"Yes."

"Yes, we are. So…I don't need to…debate with you over whether…we should do…what's best for the family. I just need to know…you're going to do it. Doesn't that make sense, sweetheart?"

"Yes."

"And you're going to do…what's best for our family?"

Van sighed. "Of course."

"Very good, dear. Now how do you propose…we go about it?"

"Ian and I will take him out through the parking garage. The desk nurse here is taken care of."

"How much did that cost us?" Mrs. Norris asked.

"Three thousand."

The old lady winced like she'd been stuck with a pin. "Three thousand dollars! You ain't got no more sense than… You'd pay five dollars…for a bucket of spit." The hateful tone she used was awful to hear. It was so much worse than the way she had spoken to me. She stared at him hard for a moment and huffed, "Some fucking lawyer…you are. First, you were supposed to get…old lady Dyess to sign over control of the…luminum plant. But you fucked that up. Then you give the preacher…a copy of the will."

"Am I going to have to hear about this for the rest of my life?" Van demanded. "It's what Ms. Dyess told me to do. Card was the only one she trusted. How was I supposed to know you and Doolittle were going to try to circumvent her will? I thought the matter was laid to rest when she died."

"Maybe if you'd actually think...for once in your damn life."

"Stop attacking me!" he snapped. He seemed to get smaller as he said it, like a balloon deflating.

Mrs. Norris titled her head.

Ian smirked. It was the first expression I'd seen drift across his long, flat iceberg of a face.

Finally Mrs. Norris smiled at Van, warmly, understandingly. "Oh, my baby," she said tenderly. She took his hand and kissed it. "You're under...so much stress. You do take care of...your momma."

"Thank you," he said dryly.

Ian didn't move. He just stood there like a machine that wasn't being used.

Mrs. Norris told Van, "I know...you'll take care of this...for me."

"I will."

"And the stuff...with the papers...and the investigators?"

Van gently pulled his hand away from his mother and put it in his pocket. "I'll take care of all of it, mother."

Mrs. Norris smiled and folded her arms in her lap. She looked like an old lady again, an old lady leaving a quilting circle.

"Ian," she said over her shoulder, "you take me...down to Dawn. She'll drive me...home. Then you come up here...and help your uncle."

Ian said, "Yes, Grandmom."

She looked at me. "Goodbye," she said. "Goodbye... mister dead man."

After Ian had rolled her out, Van leaned against the wall and slipped his hand out of his pocket. "She's crazy, of course," he said.

I didn't say anything.

He wiped a smudge of lipstick off his knuckle. "But she's my mother, I suppose."

He shook his head.

"And Ian…his parents are gone, and she raised him like you'd train a dog for pit fighting. He'd come in here and cut my throat if she told him to."

He jabbed his hand back in his pocket and jiggled his keys and chewed on his bottom lip.

"What now?" I asked.

He raised his eyes and stared at me over his glasses. "Goodbye mister dead man."

Chapter Nineteen

When Ian came back in, he was cracking his walnut-sized knuckles. "Let's get to work," he said.

Van asked, "Is it ready downstairs?"

"Yep."

They looked at me. It was a bizarre thing to watch them size me up like a broken sink.

"Should we do it here?" Ian asked.

I opened my mouth to yell *help!* and had gotten the first syllable out when, in one fluid motion, Ian leapt to the bed and struck me across the mouth. A pain shot down my neck and into my shoulders. Suddenly there was a knife in his hand. "Don't," he said. "Or we'll make it hurt. We're mostly alone on this hall, anyway. Just make it easy on both of us and be quiet."

My lip was bleeding and my teeth hurt. Ian slid the cold blade across my sweaty forehead.

Van said, "I don't have much experience with this end of it."

Ian put the knife away. "I'll handle it."

"Well then. What's the best way?"

Ian walked over to him and took his arm and they went out in the hallway. I scrambled for the phone. The movement made my neck explode with pain and it was all for nothing, anyway, because the phone was disconnected. I looked around for something, anything. In the drawer was a Bible, a pad and a pencil. I took the pencil. Maybe I could jab someone in the eye with it.

After a few minutes, Ian came back into the room. He leaned over the guard rail, a giant hovering over me, and said, "Here's the deal." His voice was like a depth charge. "I'm not a trained liar like Uncle Van. I think laying things out is best. This is the situation: You are going to die tonight. I assume you already know this."

There was nothing to say to that. There was nothing in Ian's eyes that could be appealed to. I was a master manipulator, but there was nothing there to manipulate.

Ian solemnly acknowledge my silence. "Good, you do know. You should. I don't want there to be any doubt about it. It's my job to kill you, so you know it's going to get done. And I think the best way to do it is to just dope you up and slit your throat in the bathtub. That's the way I'd do it if it was just me. But Uncle Van wants us to have you check out. He's one for the dotting of i's and crossing of t's. And it'll be all around easier if you just walk out to the SUV and get in and we drive off. He wanted me to try and trick you, some foolishness like you see in the movies. Tell you we're not going to kill you so you'll come along peacefully." He shook his block head. "You heard Grandmom. She said you're going in the ground tonight and her word is gospel. I suspect you know that. The cops are going to want you for killing the preacher and his wife and spoiling their daughter. Anyway you look at it, you're dead. So here's the offer I'm willing to make you: if you sign yourself out, and if you walk out quietly to the car, I won't hurt you. We'll go for a short ride to the family plot. I'll let you say a last prayer, smoke a cigarette or say a few last words. And then, once you're ready, it'll be a relatively peaceful death. One bullet in the back of the head. There's a chance that you won't even hear the gun. If you think about it, that isn't a bad proposition. One pop and it'll be over. Most people don't get to die that quickly or simply." He leaned in close, just as his grandmom had done, and I could smell meat on his breath. "Otherwise, I'm going to have to hurt you. And since I'm not a sadist, I'll be angry with you for making me hurt you. That's just more weight for the soul to carry. I'll torture you with the cold fury of a man who's been forced into it. Do you understand me?"

Van walked in and said, "That's enough, Ian. For Christ's sake."

Ian turned and stared at him blankly for a moment. Then he said, "It's hard to believe you and Doolittle were brothers."

"Isn't it though?" Van said. He pulled open the closet and took out my clothes. "Your church friends," he told me, "they brought some spares for you." He tossed them on the bed. "Get changed and we'll be going." He looked at Ian and jerked his head at the door. They walked to the hall to whisper some more, and I slowly got dressed.

I wasn't really thinking. My neck hurt and my left hand was wrapped to protect my broken fingers. There was blood under my fingernails and my hands were shaking. I couldn't think. Mostly, I thought about putting on my clothes. I looked down at the pencil, my would be weapon, and I dropped it on the floor, letting it roll under the bed. I was tired and my body was quivering with pain. I didn't care anymore. Why not let Ian give me one in the back of the head?

I was dressed and sitting there quietly when Ian and Van walked back in. Ian was grinning. Van looked like his head hurt.

"Let's go," he said.

Hell on Church Street

• • •

After I signed a couple of forms at the vacant nurse's station, we made our way down the hall as if nothing were wrong. Tense beside me, Van stared at the elevator at the end of the hall without blinking, but Ian strolled along as if he were wandering outside for a smoke. I walked between them. That's all. I felt numb.

One in the back of the head.

I chuckled. Ian glanced at me and drifted a little closer to me, but Van kept staring at the elevator. The halls were long, clean and pastel. And empty. It was as though the Norris reputation and money had evaporated any last vestiges of humanity. It was just me and the Norris boys.

In the elevator, Van pushed the button for the bottom floor while Ian leaned his bulk against the wall behind me. Being a medium sized county hospital, there were just four floors and a basement/parking garage. We'd been on three and were headed for the garage, but suddenly the elevator stopped on the first floor. Van shot a look at Ian.

Ian stood up straight. "Stay calm," he intoned. "Both of you."

The doors slid open and a young couple smiled at us. The girl was pregnant and the boy was carrying a powder blue baby bag.

"Hello," the girl said as they crowded onto the elevator.

"Hi," I said. "How are you?"

Ian touched my back.

"Fine," the girl said. She was a strawberry blonde with a skinny face and small legs. Her young man took her hand. I don't remember anything about him. I was looking at her, at the field of freckles spread across her nose and cheeks.

"When are you due?" I asked.

"Seventeen days," she said.

"That's wonderful. Congratulations."

Her young man stared at the digital readout of the floor numbers. She smiled quietly and said, "Thank you." She glanced at my neckbrace and said, "I hope you're okay."

The cold, flat side of a blade rubbed against my elbow.

I sighed. She was looking at me, half smiling, waiting for me to answer.

The bell dinged and the door opened.

The young man stepped out and the girl blinked and I didn't say anything and she stepped out. Van stepped out behind her, and I followed him.

"Over here," Ian said. "You need to take it easy."

"Good luck," I told the girl. "Congratulations."

She grinned at me, glanced at Ian, then back at me and said, "Thank you. I hope you're okay."

Her young man took her hand, and she smiled and turned and walked off with him.

The garage was tiny, but the young couple was parked on the side opposite Ian's SUV. Still, I could hear their footsteps behind me. Something in that slowed me down, some distant echo of hope, but Ian moved in close to me—so close we were walking in step with each other—and whispered, "If you make me hurt a pregnant girl, I'll torture you for months."

I'd love to say I remained quiet to protect the pretty young mother-to-be, but there's no point in trying to convince you that I'm a decent human being. I wasn't fearful for the girl, but when Ian attached himself to me and whispered that he'd kill her, I knew he would. It deflated me. My last hope was gone.

Climbing into the back of the SUV, I had every expectation I was about to die. And most of the time, to be completely honest, I wish I had.

Chapter Twenty

After I'd been handcuffed in the back seat, we pulled out of the garage. As we slipped off toward the mountains, Ian rolled down his window and lit a cigarette. Van sat next to him and watched me. Soon we were out of town completely and, as Ian followed the road hugging the black side of some mountain, they sat silhouetted in the moonlight and dashboard lights.

"That went well," Ian said.

"I'm glad you think so," Van said.

Ian regarded his cigarette for a moment. "You worry too much, Van. It's bad for your heart."

Van shook his head.

"What?" Ian said.

Van shook his head again.

Ian said, "What?" again.

"I have to worry," Van snapped. "I'm the only one who does. It's my job in this family. You heard what she was saying back there. That's not new. She's not coming up with fresh insults, Ian. Those insults are fifty-seven years old. She's been saying that shit my entire life, but I've always had to be the cautious one."

"It seems to me that Doolittle did pretty well looking out for himself."

Van snorted. "You really think that, don't you?"

"What?"

"You and her both…"

Ian glanced at me in the rearview mirror. He asked Van, "Are you watching him?"

Van turned and looked at me. "Yes," he said, but then he turned back to Ian and said, "You and she both act as if I'm inessential. Doolittle at least understood my function in the family."

"Grandmom runs this family."

Van sighed. "Sure."

"Well, doesn't she?"

Van rubbed his face. "Oh Doolittle," he said prayerfully, "you got off easy, man. Death is the only respite." Then to Ian he said, "She's an old woman, Ian. She's just a mean old woman. Yes, she is still as strong as a hurricane, and, yes she's crazier than the rest of us—which is saying quite a goddamn lot—but at the end of the day she's just a mean old woman."

"So who runs the family?"

"Doolittle was running the family. I was running the family."

Ian sucked on his cigarette while cold air poured through the open window. Van and I shielded ourselves from it, sat away from it, or put our shoulders to it, but Ian sat there and let it wash over him like wind across a glacier.

"You don't know what you're talking about."

"I was r—"

"Let me tell you why you don't know what you're talking about. Doolittle is gone. That means we need a new field general. Because that's what Doolittle was. He was a field general. You? You're a captain maybe. I was a captain, too. But Grandmom is the President, Van. You'll do good not to forget that."

Van turned to me and stared for a while. His thoughts revolved around something else entirely, though. Some distant concern preoccupied his mind, but I couldn't tell which troubled him, the past or the future.

Finally he told his nephew, "My point is that someone has to worry. She's reckless. It's not disloyal to point that out."

"I suppose we have different ideas about worrying, then. And recklessness."

"Well, I suppose we do, but you might consider that Doolittle trusted me. Perhaps you should, too."

"I trust her because she's my family, Van. You're a glorified business associate."

Van shook his head. "I'm as much your family as she is, Ian."

Ian laughed, something I wouldn't have thought possible. "Where were you when my father took off? Where were you when my mother died? Where was Doolittle? Uncle Leon? Where was Aunt Lacey even?"

"We all pitched in, Ian."

"Yeah," Ian said flipping his dead cigarette butt out the window. "I don't remember that. What I do remember is Grandmom."

"She wouldn't let anyone see you, Ian!" Van slid to the edge of his seat, staring at his nephew. "None of us. She kept you out here in the middle of nowhere. I'd drive out here and she'd send me away. Ask Lacey. It happened to all of us. Every time I saw you, you were an inch taller and twenty pounds heavier. We got to see you once, maybe twice a year."

"I'm sure you tried really hard."

"Ian, I'm telling you. Ask anybody. If Doo were here he'd tell you the same thing. You were this skinny five year-old boy, and she took you up here to the house and locked the door, and when you came out again you were twenty years-old and the size of a mountain."

Ian shifted in his seat. "What exactly are you trying to say to me, Van?"

Van sighed. "Nothing, Ian."

"No, tell me."

Van shook his head. "Forget it." He slumped back in his seat and stared at me. "What do you make of our little family dramas, Brother Webb?"

"Every unhappy family is unhappy in its own way."

Van stared at me a little while longer. Then he leaned back and shut his eyes and said, "That's the first time Tolstoy's been quoted in this vehicle, I'll bet." Then he was quiet.

We drove in silence for the better part of an hour. My mind, which is usually running, was calm. Or numb. I wasn't worried about dying. I wasn't thinking of heaven or hell or the Cards or Angela. I wasn't thinking of anything. We wound deeper into the dark hollers of the Ozark mountains, so that rock and a dark canopy of trees replaced the night sky. Van slept, or pretended to sleep, and Ian drove, his shoulders wide and rigid as he sat pressed over the wheel.

Finally, he turned off the two-lane blacktop, and we jostled down a dirt road. Dirt and gravel rattled against the bottom of the SUV. Sitting up, Van looked back at me. I couldn't see his face.

Ian turned off the dirt road and climbed a grassy slope into the trees. When the grass ran out at the trees he stopped the SUV.

Ian climbed into the back, slid the back door open and pulled me out. Van got out behind us. The night sky shone through the treetops, and blue moonlight soaked our skin. Ian nudged me toward the trees.

Chapter Twenty-one

I walked with the two of them at my back.

Ahead of me black trees crisscrossed their own wavering shadows like swaying prison bars. The forest swallowed me with every step I took. As the Norris family marched me through the brittle Arkansas winter woods to my death, I simply shut down. My hands were cuffed in front of me, and I lifted them to push branches aside. That was the extent of my caring.

I did think it odd that neither of the Norrises thought to get in front of me. The smartest thing, it seemed to me, would have been for Van to lead the way with me in the middle and Ian in the back. But they barely seemed aware of me.

And that, really, is the point isn't it? Even to my murderers, I was insignificant.

"What are you trying to say?" Ian's deep voice asked.

"What?" Van's voice was thin, scared of the shadows and the distant night murmurings through the trees. "I didn't say anything." Then, "Jesus, it's been a while since I've been here."

"Back in the car. What you were saying about Grandmom, about her being crazy."

"Forget it, Ian. It doesn't matter."

"It seemed to matter to you back there. That's what

worries me about you, Van. You're duplicitous. That's why she installed you as the lawyer in the family."

"I went to law school, Ian. That's why I'm a lawyer."

A gust of wind rattled the branches like talismans. "That's the other thing about you that worries me," Ian said. "You think you're your own man. An intelligent man would know better."

I stepped over a log and stumbled a bit and Ian's giant hand swallowed my elbow and straightened me.

"Keep going," he said.

I kept going, and Van said, "I am my own man, Ian. And I'm not afraid of you."

In all honesty, at that moment, I was more worried for Van than I was for myself. Like a man shouting advice at a movie screen, I wanted to warn him, wanted to tell him to shut up.

"Van," Ian said, "you shouldn't be afraid of me. You should be afraid of her."

"She's an old woman," Van said, but his voice trembled as if he were afraid she might hear him.

In front of me, the trees began to thin out, and then we were in a clearing. There wasn't much to it, just some grass and stones, all of it black and gray with night. The Norris family graveyard. My graveyard.

Van moved to my left, looking at the ground. "I haven't been here in…since that night. Since that Thanksgiving."

"The night she saved the family," Ian said, moving to my right.

Van made a sound like a laugh in the bottom of his throat. "I guess. Before that, we were an abused family. After that, we were a pack of murderers."

"You *are* weak," Ian said. "She's so right about you. You would rather have stayed a victim. You, her eldest son, would have left her a slave to the most disgusting monster that hell ever vomited into this world."

Van stood with his hands on his hips, hanging his head to contemplate the ground where his father had been rotting for decades. "I was barely seventeen years old, Ian."

Cold moonlight burned on Ian's smooth scalp and massive shoulders. From the darkness his voice, heavy and thick, said, "At seventeen, I would have died for her. I would have bled every drop of my blood before I let another man touch her."

Van pulled himself up straight and looked at Ian. "That's what she wanted. That's why she took you away from us."

"Go on, Van. Say what you want to say."

As quietly as possible, I took a single step backward. The two silhouettes faced one another like thick, heavy shadows.

"You poor dumb bastard. I'm saying she kept us away from you so she could grow you into her own little solider."

"You must be insane to talk to me this way."

"I must be."

"You, who would let a man beat her in front of you. You, who were conceived in a drunken rape."

"She told you that?" Van asked. Then he shook his head. "What am I saying? Of course, she did."

Ian squared himself even as his cavernous voice began to crack. "She told me. She told me about the night of their wedding, how her father had given her to that…man, that preacher's son who everyone loved and respected. She told me how on that first night he got drunk and beat her and used her. And she told me how you were born from that night."

"Jesus, Ian. You could have been such a good kid."

Ian was quiet a moment, but I heard a sound that might have been emotion dying in his throat. Finally he said, "You, the bastard of the monster who…raped that precious woman."

Van said, "She took you off and now she's done this. She's infected you like she infected all the ones she gave birth to. Only worse."

Ian started toward him, a colossus in the night. His voice, bewildered almost to the point of amusement, rose on a tide of anger. "You must want to die. To talk about her this way to me, you must want me to kill you."

"Ian…"

"You must want to die."

"No. I don't," Van said, and raised a gun in the darkness and shot Ian five times in the chest.

Chapter Twenty-two

I don't remember hitting the ground. I just recall the explosion and Ian's yelp, and then I was on the ground, tasting dirt and leaves.

Silhouetted against the night sky, Van stood, his arm outreached, still pointing the gun at Ian. A wisp of gunpowder floated on the breeze above me.

Ian lay on the ground, clawing at the grass. One foot dug into the dirt like he was trying to climb out of a hole. A low moan escaped him with a final breath, and then he was dead.

Van walked over to him and knelt down. For a moment, he just crouched there, staring at the big dead man. Then he felt for a pulse.

My every muscle was in disagreement as to what to do. Charge him? Run? Lay there and wait and see? Paralyzed, I did nothing. But though my body couldn't will itself to action, I did feel something. Only later, thinking back on it, was I able to decipher the feeling. And it was this: a reawaking of fear. I had thought I was ready to die out there in the woods, but then when the shooting started, I ducked.

And there you go: Nobody wants to die.

"He's dead," Van said. His voice was clear and remorseless.

I didn't say anything.

He turned around and walked over to me. I pulled myself up to my knees.

"Please," I said. "Please, Van."

He bent down, and I could finally see his pale blue face in the darkness. The gun dangled from his right hand.

"What do I do with you? That is the question."

I started to say something, but he shook his head. "No," he said. "Just get up. Let's go back to the car. No talking, though. Let me think."

I did as he said and, leaving Ian dead in the grass, together we tripped back through the darkened woods. When we got to the SUV, we climbed in without a word. Ian had left the keys in the ignition, and Van started it up and backed out of the clearing. As we bumped down the road, I tried to hold my tongue, but the fear in me was real and rising, feeding, as fear does, on the newfound hope I had. It was too much for me.

"What are you thinking?" I asked.

Van shook his head. Though he was the family lawyer, he was the only Norris I'd met who wasn't a talker. I knew I'd have to make my pitch and run the risk of irritating him.

"I'm going to be honest with you, Van," I said. "I'm not sure why you did what you just did. I can assume, that in part, it comes out of years of conflict in your family. But I also assume—I also assume that it was driven primarily by self-preservation. It was like you told your mother, killing me is a bad idea. It only draws more attention to your family."

Van drove with one hand on the wheel. The other hand, in his lap, held the gun.

"Think about this," I said. "What happens if I disappear? What happens if I go away? Won't the storm follow me? Doolittle, the Cards, all of it points at me, and if I go away it all follows after me."

"You're making a good case for getting rid of you permanently, you know."

My Adam's apple jerked, and I had to swallow before I could say, "Yes. But think of it this way: As long as I'm running, they keep chasing."

"And when they find you? Which they always do, in the end. What's to stop you from talking about what just happened?"

"Futility," I replied. "The futility of my situation. The day I don't show up to work, I'll be wanted for double homicide. And arson. And statutory rape. Maybe second degree murder for Doolittle. What would be the point of trying to sell you to the police? Even if I wanted to sell you out, who would believe me? I'd be the world's worst witness. And anyway, I know you're too smart to leave Ian out there. You'll move him. You'll have an alibi in place. I don't doubt you could have me killed in jail. Why would I bring down your wrath?"

We came to the end of the road and I was thoroughly confused about where we were. Van stopped for a moment and we were still on the road. To our left, another gravel road led up a hill into more trees, more darkness. He stared up that road for a while. I didn't know if he was contemplating taking me up there to kill me, but I was no longer numb to the thought of death. I thought of Ian, big and breathing and mean, lying out in the woods, his body stiffening in the night air. I'd survived Doolittle. I'd survived Ian. I was ready to fight Van if I needed to, and when he turned left and followed the road into the trees, my hands tightened into fists.

"Where are we going?" I asked.

"I think you are more right than you know. I'm going to turn you loose and deny I've even met you. First, though, we have to make a stop."

We crunched up the gravel road until it gave way to a

smooth dirt drive leading to a big ramshackle house. The house was two stories, with a wide front porch and big frame windows. The house was dark except for the porch light. In the distance, I could see a barn and a jumble of old vehicles rusting in the dew.

Van cut the lights and pulled up slowly near the house and sat there a moment.

He looked at the house and dug a key ring out of his pocket. He uncuffed me, and then he slid another key off the ring and handed it over to me.

I took it.

He pointed at the house. "My mother," he said.

I looked at the house.

He pointed at the furthermost upstairs window. "Up there."

He took a deep breath.

"What?" I said.

"I want you to go up there."

I stared at him.

He stared back.

"Are you saying what I think you're saying?" I asked.

"Yes."

"Your own mother?"

Van took another deep breath. "We're not exactly the Waltons, Brother Webb."

I shook my head and tried to hand the key back.

He frowned like I'd offended his intelligence. "At this late date, do you really want me to believe you have any reservations about going up there and smothering a little old lady in her bed? A little old lady who, by the way, will have us both tortured and killed if she finds out about Ian." He nodded at the key. "Go on. And keep this thought in mind: she's the worst problem you have."

"So, if I do this?"

"Then I drive us back to town. You're free to do whatever you want—though if I were you, I'd run like hell."

The weight of it started to press down on me. "I suppose Ian and your mother, both their deaths will be following me too now?"

Van smiled. I guess he couldn't help himself, but for the first time I was sure he was a Norris. "They can only execute you once, Brother Webb."

"Christ," I swore.

"It's your call. It's the best deal you are going to get, though. I let you go *and* you get my mother off your back. If she lives long enough to find out Ian is dead, she'll burn Arkansas to the ground looking for you."

"I'll do it," I said. What else could I say? I knew he was right.

Van said, "She'll be asleep by now. She's not one of those old women who stays up all night. She likes her sleep. Always has. Go in the front door, the stairs are to your left. Top of the stairs, take another left. The last room on the right. Her hearing aid will be on the table next to her teeth. Do it fast, and let's get out of here."

I squeezed my fist around the key, opened the door and got out of the SUV. I walked around the side and started up to the darkened house. Somewhere off in the woods I heard a dog, lonely and cold. The key felt heavy in my sweaty palm. I switched it to my other hand. My neck ached.

When I got to the house, I climbed the porch steps quickly. Easing the key into the front door, I looked back at Van. I could make him out in the moonlight, his face drawn and sad. I don't know what he was thinking. I suppose he assumed life hadn't given him many choices.

I knew life hadn't given me any choices. I opened the door and stepped inside.

Chapter Twenty-three

It smelled like an old woman's house. It was the smell of carpets in need of a cleaning, of shelves layered in dust, of years of meat frying in the kitchen. It was the sharp stink of cat urine. It was the accumulation of memory and age, the neglect of *now* for the comforting stupor of *then*.

I waited at the door, taking in the smell, letting my eyes adjust. I thought of being in the Cards' home. I suppose that comparison was inevitable. The difference for me, of course, was that I'd not entered the Cards' home to kill them. Despite what anyone might say, I snuck into their home to burgle it for Doolittle.

But I snuck into Bertie Mae Norris's home to kill her. That old woman was the only person I ever set out to kill.

As I stood there in her foyer, though, I was thinking less about Mrs. Norris' life and more about her house. When I'd snuck into the Card home, I knew my way around. I'd been there. But I'd never stepped foot in Mrs. Norris's home in my life. Van's instructions slipped past me like a tossed off phone number.

I knew I was looking for stairs. As my eyes adjusted to the house's mix of darkness and moonlight, I could tell that the foyer led into a large den. There were a couple of sofas, a coffee table, a painting over a hearth. To my right, hints of moonlight slanted through some kitchen windows and shone down on a cat sitting on the counter. He stared at me, unagitated but not altogether uninterested. The shadows beneath the table moved.

It was another cat. A fat one. He strolled across the kitchen's hardwood floors and walked up to me, nuzzling my leg. I reached down to pet him, and he twisted his head into my palm and plopped down on the floor at my feet as if he'd loved me his entire life.

I stood up and moved to my left. The cat watched me go, stood up and wandered back into the kitchen. To my left there was a flight of steps, surprisingly steep. Gently, I took the first step, but the boards groaned like I had pained them. Ian might have been completely devoted to his grandmom, but he hadn't spent his time keeping the house up for her. Van had said that his mother was a heavy sleeper, but every step I took creaked. Halfway up, another cat spat at me, clawed at my leg and darted down the stairs. I had to grab the railing to keep from tumbling backwards.

At the top of the steps, I took a moment. There were no windows in the hallway, and I couldn't remember where Van had told me to find his Mother. I went left, creeping down the hall. Another goddamn cat hissed at me. It was scrawny, with a clipped tail and an arched back.

I tried to move past it, but the damn thing kept hissing, its hiss getting louder and building into a loud, awful growl.

I wanted to run. I didn't want the old woman to wake up and start screaming. I didn't want to have to look her in the eyes.

The cat kept growling. I stuck my foot out, just shook it in the direction of the goddamn beast. The cat took a couple of swipes at my shoe and I kicked it in the face. It darted away, thumped into a wall and ran away.

After I'd caught my breath, I went to the end of the hall.

Mrs. Norris's bedroom was facing the front yard, so I knew it had to be on the right. The door was closed.

When I turned the doorknob, my hand was slick with sweat. The door creaked like an old casket. I stepped inside. Directly in front of me a lot of moonlight shone through two big windows a few feet apart. It took a couple of long seconds for my eyes to adjust. I wasn't even sure where the bed was. When my eyes settled down, I saw the big bed between the windows. I also saw Mrs. Norris sitting up and staring at me, cold moonlight glinting off the gun in her hand.

"You come up here…to kill me?"

I didn't have any way to answer that question, so I didn't even try.

"That's my…son out there…in the truck?"

"Yes ma'am," I said.

As my eyes adjusted, I saw her hair draped down both sides of her chest. She was wearing a white nightshirt and in the dark she looked a great deal younger. It took a second—because she'd surprised me, because she had a gun, because I was terrified—but I also noticed something else. It's another of those details which did not register so much at the time, but which the years have brought clarity to: she was sitting on the left side of the bed, not in the middle. To her right was a dent in the mattress. A big dent.

"Where's Ian?" she asked.

I felt for the door.

She held the gun up with both hands. "I'm old," she said, "but this here's an easy…gun to shoot. And…I found the bullets for it…when I got home…So you take your hand… off the door."

I dropped my hand. "Okay," I said.

"Now, I asked you…a question."

"I don't know."

"I know you're lying, dear. You tell me…where my Ian is."

"Please," I said. I didn't know what else to say.

She stared at me. I couldn't see her well, but I think she might have had tears in her eyes. "Ian…"

"It wasn't me," I said.

She lowered the gun. Her head drooped. I could have run. I knew it, but I didn't run. I watched her sit there in the dark contemplating Ian. "My precious Ian."

"It wasn't me," I said.

"No," she said leaning back into her pillows. "It was Van. That took my precious Ian."

"Yes ma'am," I said. "He was the one who sent me up here." I was getting my steam back. I could run, but I saw more benefit in not running at that moment. "I don't know why he killed Ian." I started talking then. I told her I could go back downstairs, tell Van I'd done what he wanted me to do. She could be one step ahead of him. Or she could go out with me and confront him. Or I could lure him into the house. I talked for a while. I spun it. I sold it to her.

And she said nothing. She didn't move. At all.

It took me a while to notice. I get caught up in hearing myself talk, as you've doubtless realized. But it finally did break through. She wasn't moving. I said, "Mrs. Norris."

Nothing.

"Mrs. Norris?"

I took a step forward. The gun in her lap still glinted in the moonlight. I grabbed it. And she sat there, her head back in the pillow, her eyes opened. I touched her shoulder and she slumped back a little, her lungs releasing the last breath she had taken, a breath trapped there as she had slumped over and died.

• • •

"Well?" her son asked as we pulled out of the yard.

"She's dead," I said. "Your mother is dead."

Van put his elbow on the arm rest of his seat and rubbed his face. When we got to the end of the gravel road, he turned and we went down another gravel road until we hit the two lane black top.

We were driving for a while in silence when he coughed and wiped some tears away and cleared his throat.

"You must find that pretty funny," he said. "The fact that I'm crying."

I watched him for a while as he wiped away more tears and stopped crying altogether. I thought of his mother dying of a broken heart, thought of Brother Card's scream when he saw his wife dead on their kitchen floor, thought of Angela sobbing over the loss of her parents.

I shook my head. "Everybody loves somebody."

Chapter Twenty-four

Van drove back to the hospital and pulled up to the curb, far from the entrance.

"Here?" I asked.

"Where else?"

"I thought you'd take me back to Church Street."

"No," he said. "It does neither of us any good to be seen together."

"How am I going to get home?"

I didn't mean anything by the question, but Van looked at me with pity. "Jesus," he said. "You're certainly a puzzle to me, Brother Webb. For a criminal mastermind, you are certainly clueless."

"I'm not a criminal mastermind."

"No, but you are a criminal. As am I. You can get out now. We won't be seeing each other again, of course. I'd recommend you start running as quickly and smartly as you can."

I opened the door and got out. I didn't have anything left to say, nor did he, so he drove off and I walked back up to the hospital. I had to get back to Little Rock, but I didn't have any money on me. I figured I'd go to the nurses' station and use their phone to call someone from the church.

I was still thinking that when I heard someone call my name.

I turned and saw Brother Herschel walking out one of the side doors to the hospital. I waved at him.

Then I noticed he was with Nick.

They walked over to me, and Nick asked, "Was that Van?"

"Pardon?"

"The guy that just dropped you off. It looked like my brother-in-law."

"Yeah, that was Van. We were talking."

Brother Herschel smiled at me. "I'm surprised to see you up and about so soon, Brother," he said.

I rubbed my shoulder. "Sore," I said, "but okay. I'm a quick healer. Always have been."

They offered to give me a lift home. I didn't particularly want to talk to Nick, but I needed to get to the house as soon as possible so I accepted. I kept checking behind us to see if there was anyone following Nick's car. Occasionally, trucks or cars would appear, but I didn't see any signs we were being followed. Not that I could have known, I guess.

Nick drove, and Brother Herschel sat up front so I could sprawl out in the backseat. I actually fell asleep for a little while. Exhausted, I just passed out.

I dreamed. I'm not much of a dreamer, really. I never have been. Maybe my subconscious is too underdeveloped, or maybe there's just not enough going on inside of me. I don't know, but I rarely dream. The dream I had in Nick's backseat disturbed me. I was in my father's house. He sat on the back porch shooting at the trees. Angela and I hid in my room and she showed her breasts to me, but she had no nipples.

My father called, "Angela!"

"I have to go," she said.

"No," I said.

And then she was Bertie Mae Norris and she leaned over

and kissed me. My mouth was bloody. I pushed her away and ran outside. Angela was sitting on Brother Card's lap. I stood behind them. In the yard, Mrs. Card was picking up fallen limbs. I started to cry and woke up.

As soon as he saw that I was awake, Nick was ready with the questions.

He said, "I wasn't aware that you knew the Norris family."

He was talking, of course, about Doolittle. It took me a second, as I tried to shrug off the dream, to remember what Nick knew and did not know.

"Not very well," I replied. "I didn't know them until you introduced me to Sheriff Norris. You remember? His son is in our youth group."

"That's right," he said.

"We had done some talking over the last few weeks about..." I could not remember Tim's name "about his son. I think it had opened up an avenue for witnessing. We were talking about it here and there. I think the Lord was convincing him that he needed a change."

Brother Herschel nodded.

Nick glanced at me in the rearview mirror. "I see," he said. "It's odd that Doolittle didn't mention anything to Lacey about that."

"How is Lacey? It must be a hard time for her."

"Well, her brother is dead, and we have no reason to think that his soul was saved before he died..." Nick's tone implied that I was an idiot. Or worse.

"I'm so sorry. Please tell her."

"Odd that Doolittle wouldn't tell her about this struggle he was having," Nick said. "She and I have been trying to talk to him about the Lord for the last eight years, so it's really bizarre that he wouldn't mention it to her, don't you think?"

"I don't think he wanted to tell her yet. It was a disturbing thing for him, I suppose. He wasn't a man given to examining his life."

"No," Nick said. "He certainly wasn't."

"So we were talking. Just riding around and talking."

"I came to see you a few days ago. Saw Van there. And Ian lurking around. Do you know them well?"

"Not very well. Just met them…as a result of this tragedy. Van, I believe, is a lawyer of some kind."

"I believe," Brother Herschel said, "he has some unsavory connections. That's what I've been led to believe, anyway."

Nick said, "His primary unsavory connection was Doolittle. I only see Van a couple of times a year. I don't know Ian at all. He lives up in the mountains with his grandmother. No one sees either of them very much."

"Tight family," I said.

"Not really my family," Nick shot back.

"No," I said.

Nick watched me in the rearview mirror for a moment and he said, "I'd like to ask you something."

I leaned back. "I need to rest," I said.

Brother Herschel nodded, the old peacemaker. "I agree," he said. "We should let the man rest his bones, Nick."

Nick didn't say anything more, but when we rolled into my driveway an hour later he walked me to the porch. I unlocked the front door, and Nick stood there watching me.

"Thanks for the lift," I said.

He straightened up like he was reporting for duty at a flagpole. "I should tell you," he said, "that there has been some disturbing talk around the church the last few days."

"About what?"

"About you. Brother Herschel's too polite to mention anything. I'm not so polite. I'm direct. Do you care if I'm direct with you right now, brother?"

I leaned against the door. "No, Nick," I said. "Please be direct."

"Gabriel Card brought it to my attention that his sister met with you at the school near his aunt's house a few days ago."

"Yes."

He cocked his head a little. "Is there anything else about that meeting that you feel is relevant?"

I pursed my busted bottom lip and said, "No. I'm her pastor. Is there anything odd about a youth pastor meeting with a youth who has gone through a traumatic loss?"

"If the meeting takes place in private."

"It was hardly in private. It was in a public place, a public place she called and asked me to meet her at. You yourself encouraged me to talk to her. I don't see that Gabe has a cause for concern."

Nick glared at me. "Gabe seems to think there was something going on between the two of you."

I glared back at him as long as I could, then I rattled my keys a little and stared down at them.

"Preposterous," I said.

"She came to see you at the hospital," he said.

"So did you."

"There are no rumors going around about me and you, though," he said.

"Have you talked to her?" I asked.

Nick crossed his arms like a disapproving father, "Yes, I've asked Angela, and, no, she has nothing to say. Her friends all seem to think there's something wrong with her, however."

"For heaven's sake, Nick, her parents were just murdered."

"They seemed to think there was something going on before that."

"I don't know what you expect me to say."

"For starters, I'd expect you to look me in the eye and tell me nothing was going on between you and Angela Card."

I looked up at him and said, "There was nothing going on between me and Angela Card."

Nick raised his thick eyebrows. "I see," he said dryly.

"God," I said, "you really don't like me, do you?"

"There's just been some disturbing talk in the last few days. I don't know what to make of it. I really don't. I'm still thinking about it, trying to figure it all out. And now this thing with Doolittle… And then, just tonight, I've seen you with Van. It's all very…"

"What?" I said. "'It's all very' what?"

Nick squared his shoulders. "It's suspicious, Geoffrey. It's all pretty damn suspicious."

"Maybe you should pray about it."

Nick stared at me like he'd like to punch me in the face. "I am praying about it. A lot of people are praying about it."

"Good," I said. "It's good to know you wouldn't rush to crucify a man on innuendo and lies."

Nick said, "I'm asking you not to speak to Angela until this is resolved."

"I see. And why is that? Doesn't that already sound like I've been convicted?"

"It's for the best. Her aunt agrees. When she took Angela to see you in the hospital she hadn't been made aware of the situation in its fullness."

"Did you make her aware of the situation in its fullness, Nick?"

"Yeah, Geoffrey. I did."

"I see."

Nick smiled. The son of a bitch smiled. I was like a butterfly with a pin through its thorax. He said, "We'll be talking later."

I stared at him for too long before I finally managed to say, "Okay."

He turned to walk back to the car.

I called to him, "You never liked me, Nick."

He turned around part ways and said, "It's not about you and me, brother. That's maybe part of the problem: you think it's about you and me." Then he kept walking.

Brother Herschel was staring at me through the windshield, his amiable old face as blank as a burlap sack. I waved. He didn't wave back.

Chapter Twenty-five

I was standing in the center of my living room. I just stood there like an idiot. My neck hurt like all hell, but I didn't take any medicine. I just stood there, thinking, but it was like trying to think at the epicenter of an earthquake. The Cards were dead; Doolittle Norris was dead; Ian and his mother were dead; the church was about to kick me out; and Angela, sweet Angela, seemed to be afraid of me. It was all falling apart, and it was all falling apart so goddamn fast I could barely keep up with it.

There wasn't any hope of pulling the church back together, not with an investigation of Doolittle's wreck and certainly not with rumors about me and the preacher's underage daughter. Jesus. If Nick knew, then I could be goddamn sure everyone knew. He'd been looking for something to get me out of the way, and I had handed it to him, two or three times more than he needed.

And of course none of that shit mattered anyway—and by *that shit* I mean my whole damn life—because I still had to deal with Van Norris. He had let me go, but it all seemed too easy. Was I being set up to take the fall for Ian and Bertie Mae Norris? Almost certainly. Would it matter that I hadn't killed either of them? I doubted it. I'd still go down for Ian's murder. And that was only if Van decided to let the law catch me. I was still dangerous to him. I ran to the window and looked out on Church Street. It was quiet, but he could already have people on the way. Or maybe the cops were on *their* way to question me about Doolittle and the Cards. Either way, if I stayed in Arkansas, I was a dead man. Jesus, the best option I had, if absolutely everything went right, was to get defrocked and thrown into jail as a statutory rapist.

I rushed into the bedroom. I didn't think about it. I didn't think about anything for days. From here on out I was going on instinct.

I threw some clothes and utilities in a little suitcase my grandmother had given me and piled in a couple of my movies. Then I cleaned out my Just-in-Case fund from a box of macaroni and cheese in the back of the cupboard. The fund only amounted to a couple hundred dollars. I would have to hit the ATM on the way out of town and clear out my account. If my last car payment check hadn't been cashed yet, I had around eight or nine hundred dollars in the bank. I'd need it all. I pulled on a coat and stuck Mrs. Norris's gun in one pocket, and my grandmother's fancy carving knife and its sheath into the coat's lining. I cursed the money situation. Brother Card had convinced me to put a bunch of cash into a CD. Sound investment, he'd called it. Good stewardship of the Lord's blessing. Asshole. Now I'd be on the run with a thousand dollars.

When I was packed and ready to go, I took one last look around the house.

I went to the back door and eased it open. I peeked around and, sensing no one, crept out. The air was sharp and cold, the same way it had been when Ian and Van led me into the woods. I was above the cold, above the pain in my chest and bones. Adrenaline pushed me forward. I kept below the sill of the living room windows and snuck around to the front of the house. There was no car. No truck. No SUV. No one was watching the house.

I got in my car and was off. I could have left town right then and who knows what might have happened? But I drove to Angela.

It's hard to tell you how I felt about her right then. I wasn't thinking of love, and I wasn't thinking of lust. But I was scared. I guess I just wanted someone with me.

When I got there, I didn't see her aunt's car in the driveway. I pulled up and sat for a second. I was too scared to get out of the car. I was too scared to drive away.

Then the front door opened, and she walked out. Her thick coat was buttoned up to her neck, and she was wearing a sock cap. I rolled down the window.

"What are you doing?" she asked.

"I came to see you," I said.

"I heard you got out of the hospital," she said. "I wanted to see you," She looked around as if someone might be watching.

"What are you doing?" I said.

"I just told you."

"No, why are you looking around?"

She held up her palms. "You're acting weird. What are you doing?"

"Come on," I said. I motioned her toward the passenger seat.

"Now where are you going?"

"We can't talk out here. Get in the car. I'll tell you while we drive around."

"I don't want to get in the car with you."

I said, "I'm freezing, Angela. My neck hurts. And I'm in trouble. Please get in the car, so we don't have to talk out here."

"Why don't we go in the house?"

"Because we can't, baby. Please get in. I haven't talked to you in days, and that's all I've wanted to do."

She looked around again. I watched her. I could always read her, and it was all there on her face. The pull. I was her first and only lover. I was all she really had left after her parents died, and despite everything she might think or fear, she desperately wanted to believe me and love me. I could still make this happen.

She closed her eyes for a moment, opened them and came around the car and got in.

As she got in, I didn't look around to see if the neighbors were peeking out their windows. They probably were. I knew that. The news that I was running off with the Card girl would tear through town like a virus. The church would know, and the cops would know. Everything was ash.

"We have to leave town," I said.

I backed out and started down the street.

"I'm not leaving town," she said flatly. She sounded like she was forty years old. "You can stop right now if you think you're taking me out of town."

I rubbed my face. We slid past the edge of the neighborhood. A few minutes later we passed a church, and I shook my head.

She was looking at me, and it was impossible to drive and read her face at the same time, but it felt like she was concerned about me.

"Are you okay? Your neck?"

"It hurts." I showed her the splints on my left hand. "Three broken fingers."

"What happened?"

I shook my head. I knew I could make this happen. I could feed her a story and make her believe it. I could still pull it off. But I needed energy. I needed desire. And right then I was empty. I was scared. I couldn't pull it off.

She looked in the backseat and saw the suitcase.

"You're running away?"

"Yes," I said.

"Why are you leaving?" she asked me.

"Some people want to kill me," I said. "Some other people are talking about me and you. Some other people want to put me in jail. A lot of people are looking to do a lot of things to me."

"People know about us?"

"Didn't you tell them?"

She frowned. "I told my brother."

On another night I might have been able to roll with that news. But I was tired and scared and hurting. "That was stupid," I said.

"Don't call me stupid."

"That was incredibly fucking stupid."

"Don't call me stupid. I'm not stupid. You think I am, but I'm not."

"Then why would you tell your fucking brother about us? How did that seem like a good idea?"

"I never heard you talk that way before, using the F-word."

I shook my head. I wished I hadn't picked her up now. "That's what you're worrying about? At a time like this, you're concerned about my cussing?"

She sat, silent and thinking. "Where are we going?" she asked.

"I'm driving around. Don't worry. I'm not about to kidnap you. I don't know what you think of me, but I'm not going to force you to leave town against your will. You can stay here with your brother and Nick and all the other assholes at the church."

"You say that like they're a bunch of bad people," she said.

"Aren't they?"

"They're all better than you," she grunted. I drove past a trailer park and down a lonely corridor of trees.

"That's nice," I said. "Now you hate me."

She looked behind us. "Where are we going?"

"Nowhere. I told you, I'm just driving around."

We passed a tiny salvage yard out there in the middle of nowhere, and then there was nothing but trees holding up the overburdened starry sky.

Angela stared at my headlights coldly tunneling into the darkness before us. "I want to go home," she said.

"I'll take you home."

"Stop the car," she demanded, but her voice was wobbling a bit. "Turn around and take me home right now."

"Don't be that way," I said. "Relax. I have some things I think we need to talk about."

She stared at me, chewing at the inside of her mouth. "Where are you taking me?"

"I'm not taking you anywhere. We're driving around, talking."

Before I knew what had happened, she started to cry.

"Why are you crying?"

"Because you're scaring me. You just keep driving even though I told you I want to go home."

"Now you're just being stupid," I told her. "Nothing bad is going to happen to you. You know I wouldn't hurt you. You know that, right?"

She looked behind us but there was nothing back there but darkness and the red glow of my taillights. She started to cry harder. It frustrated me.

"You need to stop that," I told her.

"I'm not mad at you anymore, okay? Please, just take me home."

"Why do you keep crying? Christ. Get a hold of yourself."

"Please take me home," she said. "I won't tell anybody I saw you. I'll tell Gabe and Nick I was lying."

"Nick?"

She shook her head.

"Did you talk to Nick?"

"No."

"You just said his name. Why did you just say his name? You said Gabe and Nick."

"I didn't tell him anything. I told Gabe, and I think he told Nick. But maybe he didn't, maybe he didn't."

I punched the steering wheel. "Goddamn it!" I yelled. "Why would you do that? Everything I've done was so we could be together. There are people after me. The Norris family. Do you know who they are? They're Sheriff Norris's family, and do you know why they're after me? Do you? Because I killed him, Angela. I didn't mean to, but I killed him to protect us. He wanted to tell everyone about me and you."

She sobbed now, holding her face in her hands. "Please," she said.

"But you already did. You told Gabe and Nick."

She wobbled out *please* again. It was getting irritating.

"Why are you afraid?" I demanded.

"Please…" She was trembling. "I shouldn't be here. They said I shouldn't see you again. I shouldn't be here."

"Why are you afraid of me, Angela? Talk to me. What are you afraid of? What do you think you know? What kind of ideas has Nick been giving you?"

She was still trying to say *please* but it wouldn't come out because of her crying. Slowly, she started to hyperventilate. Within a few seconds she was huffing and gasping for air.

"For Christ's sake, stop it," I said. "Just take a deep breath and let's have a conversation about all of this. Did you hear what I just told you?"

When she squeaked out another *please* I shouted, "Jesus!" and swung over to the side of the road and threw the car in park. Dust swam in my high beams.

Her breathing got worse, like she was dying.

"Stop doing that!"

"Please," she coughed.

"Stop saying 'please' like I'm doing something bad to you. You slow down and tell me why you're so upset. We can figure this out together. You think you know something terrible, don't you? But you don't. You've gotten bad information and you've listened to the wrong people and none of it, *none of it*, is true. They all just want to steal the church away from me. They want to steal you away from me."

She took a deep breath and closed her eyes.

"Good," I said. "Now open your eyes and look at me."

She opened her eyes. She looked at me.

I don't know what I thought she was going to see. Maybe I was hoping she'd open her eyes, look at me and see how much, despite all the bad things that had happened, I truly loved her.

But when she opened her eyes and fixed them on me, I knew in an instant I had lost her. She turned white, blank, emptied of Angela and filled with a horror of me. In that instant, her face seemed to absorb all my sins. It was like looking into a mirror for the first time and discovering you're a monster.

She fumbled the door open and fell out of the car. I scrambled out of my seat. Neither of us made a sound. We were past words. By the time I got outside, she was already running, her footsteps crunching in the grass leading to the woods. We ran in the pale headlights, her long, frantic shadow flickering across the trees. As I got closer to her, my shadow swallowed hers.

I caught her at the edge of the woods. Turning around she screamed and punched me in the face. The pain shot down my neck and down my back and into my stomach and groin. As I collapsed in the damp leaves, she started running again. I forced myself up and started after her. It wasn't easy. But her sock cap had slipped off and her hair was flowing behind her, and I grabbed her hair and pulled her down.

I pulled out the knife. She wailed and kicked and bit at me, but I stabbed her three times in the chest and that was all there was. The third time I really got her, and she stopped fighting and just lay there and bled to death. It took a while, and we lay in the freezing ditch and she died fast, but not as fast as her parents. Her head was tilted back in the mud, and her last cold breaths spurted out. They got shorter. The final one was only a wisp that curled off her upper lip and dissipated in the night air.

I lay there for a few moments after she was gone and stared at my own breath. Finally I got up. I pulled the knife out of her, and it caught on her coat. I had to work it out and cut myself in the process. Not bad, but I opened the skin on the back of my left hand.

I cleaned the knife off on her coat and left her there, on her back, staring up at the cloudless night sky, that endless expanse of shivering stars.

Part Three: The Worst Man in the World

Chapter Twenty-six

"And that's all there is," Webb told me. In the light from the dashboard, his face was a pale green and his eyes were black. "I disappeared after that. I cleaned out my bank account and drove west, staying to backroads, parking in the woods during the day, driving at night. I heard about myself on the radio a few days after I left town. My name, description, and the make and model of my car. At first it was assumed that Angela had run off with me, but in the early morning on the third day of my escape her body was discovered by convicts out picking up trash. I drove and drove, swapping license plates a couple of times, taking it slow and safe, gassing up at night and avoiding people whenever I could. I finally wound up outside of a dirty little town in Texas. There weren't a lot of prying eyes, but I knew I was I taking too big a risk keeping my car. So I drove out to the woods, buried the license plates and burned the inspection sticker and insurance papers. Then I covered the car in limbs. It was a long walk to the nearest town to get a Greyhound but that only increased my chances of the car going undetected for a while. When I did find a bus, I rode west."

"Why are we back in Arkansas?"

It was the first thing I'd said in a long while, and my voice cracked when I said it. There was something weird about hearing myself again. We had been in Arkansas for a couple of hours, sliding in from Oklahoma, past the foothills of the Ozark Mountains where, I guess, Doolittle Norris had tried to kill Webb. We had driven through Little Rock, a small city by a small river. Then he'd taken an exit, and we were in some shitty section on the outskirts of the city. Nothing but fast food joints, pawn shops and check cashing places.

We passed a billboard, with a big cartoon dollar bill on it, that read: FREE BUCKS BACK.

"Why would you come back here?" I asked. This time my voice didn't crack.

"I'm coming to that in a minute," he said. "I grew a beard, dyed my hair blond and dressed like a beggar. I became a beggar with Bertie Mae's gun and a little under a thousand dollars in my pocket. I drifted. I don't know how it is with other fugitives, but I never had much trouble avoiding the cops. I just stayed out of the way. I ate when I had to, drifted from here to there, slept during the day and only came out at night. Somewhere in southern California a bum beat me up and took the gun and some of my money, but I had the majority of it in a sock. Most people just looked the other way when they saw my dirty, shambling form swaying up the street in front of them.

"Everyday I worried about being caught, but then one afternoon I was sitting outside a little truck stop eating a candy bar I'd found half finished in a dumpster when I overheard a radio news report from a mini-van at the curb. The man driving the mini-van was airing up his tire while his wife and kids were inside loading up on pork rinds and Mountain Dew. His door was open and the announcer on the radio said my car had been found and positively identified in a three car pile up in the desert near Twenty Nine Palms. The body inside was believed to be mine.

"It took me a while to get the whole story, but the way

I understand it some drifter stumbled across my car, took a try with starting it, was probably shocked to find that it worked and rode off into the sunset. And then somewhere around the Marine base in Twenty-Nine Palms he got into a terrible wreck and burned to death."

"You're lucky as hell," I said. "I've never been that lucky in my life."

"Well, yes, at first I greeted the news as a miracle, but I haven't even gotten to the lucky part yet. Of course, they figured out pretty quickly it wasn't me in the car. But then the damnedest thing happened. It turned out the guy in the car was wanted for a couple of murders in Nevada. When the cops found my blood in the car, from where I had cut myself the night I killed Angela, they assumed I'd been hacked up somewhere. They probably kept looking for a while, but they wrote me off pretty quickly.

"After the first year or so, after the fire and the dead body in the car, I finally stopped running and I wound up in the north. That's when I started to live like a termite. It doesn't matter where a termite lives. I stayed in the dark, and I consumed. I replaced ambition with food. I consumed cheap food by the truckload and got fat and smoked cigarettes and watched pornography and lived in a state of filthy poverty."

"How long have you been doing this?"

"Years."

"So why are you here now?"

"Because a couple of nights ago I saw Oscar."

"Oscar...the kid Angela had the crush on?"

Webb nodded. "In a crappy corner of a dark little nothing city a thousand miles from Arkansas, he walked right in the front door of the supermarket I work at."

"Maybe he didn't notice you."

Webb shook his head. "He looked right at me. It took him a moment, but he put it together. I didn't recognize him at first, either. The last time I saw him, he was a teenager. He's a grown man now, with thinning hair and the beginnings of a paunch. We had one of those awkward moments where you know you know someone but you can't quite place them. And then he smiled that dumb alabaster smile, and it clicked for me. Oscar. Stupid, handsome Oscar. And at the same instant, beneath the beard and the fat and the distance of years and worry on my face, he recognized me."

"Sure he recognized you? Did he say anything?"

"Nothing, but I could tell he recognized me. We only met once, years ago, but I murdered a girl he went to school with. I murdered her parents and the county sheriff. Now, think of it from his point of view. He once met *Geoffrey Webb*, the cold-blooded serial killer being hunted across Arkansas and Texas on the news, and he shook my hand. He probably tells the story at parties—'How I Met The Killer At Church.' When he saw me at the store, he turned white and his smile dropped like a guillotine. He hustled out the door pretty quick, and I expect he was on the phone before he got to his car."

"What did you do?"

"I took off my apron and left out the back door. I ran."

"When was that?"

"A couple of days ago. I've been running since then. Thinking. Thinking for the first time in years. I had shut down my brain, shut down my life, turned myself into nothing but a mouth and a distended stomach. But then Oscar walked in the door and I thought, 'Oh, Jesus, that's Oscar.' And since I had that horrible thought, my mind has been like a boat taking on water. Everything started to sink, and it's been sinking ever since. Now that the police know I'm alive, they'll be looking for me, and they won't stop this time until they find me."

He turned onto Church Street. It was a nicer part of town, more residential. Little houses and yards. After a while, we passed Higher Living Baptist. It was smaller than I'd pictured it. Hard to believe, looking at the chipped steeple and ratty sign out front, that you'd murder someone to get control of such a place. But I guess people have been killed for less.

He stopped at a red light. Somewhere around here he had murdered the entire Card family. People here knew him. If Oscar really had recognized him, they'd all know about it here. It would be on the news. The cops might even be looking for this car right now. The light turned green and a chill ran down my back. I'd put away my gun a few hours ago, but now I took it out again and started tapping it against my thigh.

He drove away from town. The houses got farther and farther apart. Soon we were driving along a dark corridor of trees.

"I thought I could live like a termite," he said. "I thought that was my punishment. To live like a bug. But then Oscar showed up, and I realized I couldn't even live like that anymore."

"What are you going to do?"

"That remains to be seen," he said. "'Conscience does make cowards of us all.'"

"Say what?"

He shook his head. "Nothing. Just quoting something that has no meaning. I don't really want to die, but I don't really want to live, either." He turned down another road. We were in the middle of nowhere. "So some way or another, this has to end."

"What do you mean?"

He slowed down and pulled onto the shoulder of the road. We crunched over some gravel, and then he stopped in the grass.

He put the car in park. "This is it," he said. He leaned up and stared through the windshield. "I think it is, anyway. Of course, it was late and I wasn't in the best frame of mind at the time."

He cut the engine and got out of the car. I climbed out behind him, the gun at my side. He turned around and jerked his fleshy chin at the wallet in my other hand. "There's three thousand dollars and some change in there," he said.

I slipped the wallet into my pocket and said, "Okay." I glanced around like someone might be watching.

The black two-lane road had disappeared in the dark, and now trees boxed us in on every side.

He looked up at the stars and took a deep breath.

"This is where she died?" I asked.

Still looking at the stars he answered, "Where I killed her, yes."

"So why are you here?"

"I want to die here."

I just stared at him.

He said, "It seems fitting. I certainly deserve to die, don't I?"

"Sure," I said.

"Okay."

I kept staring at him.

"Why bring me here?" I said finally.

"I think you know."

"That's why you brought me here, to do it for you?"

"Of course."

"Why me?"

"Why not? You were ready to kill me a few hours ago for

the money in my wallet. Fine. I gave it to you."

He didn't flinch.

"You could easily do it," he said.

That's where he was wrong. I'd never actually killed anybody before. Slapping a guy around and telling him you'll blow his brains out is easy. I'd been doing it off and on for years.

This was something else, though. My hand was shaking—I didn't want him to see it, but my hand was shaking so bad I could barely hold onto the gun.

He said, "Your hand is shaking."

"Doesn't matter," I snapped. "You can do what you're going to do. I don't need a murder wrap hanging over me."

He stared back at me so hard I had to look away, and then his eyes brightened a little and he said, "Do you know it just sunk in? I get it now. It took me a while because I'm exhausted, but... You're a fake, aren't you?"

"What?"

"You're just a thug. You kick the shit out of mouthy rednecks, and you tell yourself it means something. But you're just a cut rate Saturday night badass. You're scared, and you're all talk."

"Fuck you, man. Just because I don't want to put my head in the noose for you..."

"Rationalize it how you want. You're a fake. I was always a bad man pretending to be a good man, but you're something more pathetic than that. You're an ordinary man pretending to be bad."

He laughed at me and turned and walked back to the car.

For a moment everything around us was quiet, like the whole world had died. All I could hear was my breathing and his feet stomping in the grass.

He opened the car door and white light split the field

like a sheet. I stared at the ground. Angela died right here, bleeding to death in the frozen grass, staring up at the sky.

When he shut the door, the field snapped back into darkness.

"You feel bad?" I asked over my shoulder. "About Angela, I mean. You feel guilty about what you did to her?"

Webb returned holding a gun. That got my attention.

"Bought this from a guy at work a couple of years ago," he said. "I had the idea that I might shoot it out with the cops when the day came." He held it with both hands, like an artifact. "Silly notion, really."

I kept my eye on the gun.

Webb took a long hard breath. He started to unbutton his shirt. "The hell of it is," he said, "I've never really felt guilty about anything in my life. Not really. For whatever reason, I just…never have." He pulled off his dress shirt and dropped it on the ground. "That's why I could never ask for forgiveness. From God, I mean. The world's a hellhole. What is there to forgive?"

I didn't have anything to say to that.

"I'm leaving," I said. Still holding on to my piece, I dug out his wallet and pocketed all the cash except for a hundred dollar bill. Then I threw the wallet to him. "Put that in your coat. I don't want the cops thinking you got knocked off in a robbery, even for a little while."

He just dropped the wallet on the ground and said, "You don't really think I'm going to let you leave here, do you?"

"What?"

"What's your name?"

I was about to tell him to fuck off when he raised the gun and pointed it at me.

"Your name?"

"Paul."

He said something but blood started pounding in my ears and I missed it.

"You don't got any reason to kill me," I said. My hand was sweaty and the gun felt like a cinder block.

He took a step toward me. "Everyone dies, Paul. Even Jesus died. Death's never needed a reason." He gestured at the gun hanging useless in my hand. "You got any bullets in that thing?"

"Yes," I said.

Sweat dripped in my eyes, and I wiped it away with my free hand. I could see his face in the blue moonlight. I needed to piss.

"Don't be afraid," he said. "Lift your gun."

"Why?"

"You want to leave this field alive?" he asked.

"Yes."

"You'll have to earn it."

With his free hand, he peeled off his undershirt. I took a step back.

"What are you doing?"

He kicked off his shoes and dropped his pants and boxers. His belly hung down to his thighs. "Ashes to ashes and dust to dust," he said.

Keeping the gun on me, he knelt in the grass naked as a baby.

I didn't move. "Why would you make me do this?"

"You wanted to be a bad man, Paul. Well, here's your chance. Starting tonight, you can quit pretending."

"I'm not a fucking murderer."

"You will be. You'll either leave this field a murderer or a corpse."

He dropped his arm to his side.

I hesitated. I took a deep breath.

He grimaced and started to raise his arm.

I pointed the gun at his chest and pulled the trigger and the bullet exploded so loudly I pissed myself. My eyes snapped shut and my ears rang, but I could hear him moaning in the grass in front of me. I stepped back, and he started crying. The night air suddenly stank like gunpowder and blood. When I opened my eyes, he was clawing at the grass.

I left him dying in the middle of that field and ran up the road. The blacktop stretched out in the moonlight and snaked over a hill. Blood pounded in my ears. I ran up the hill, and his cries and moans chased me like an angry dog. They only got stronger the harder I ran. By the time I got to the top, Webb was screaming like a man on fire.

ABOUT THE AUTHOR

Jake Hinkson is a native of the Arkansas Ozarks. He is a regular contributor to the film journal *Noir City*, and he writes about crime fiction and film at *CriminalElement.com*. He currently resides in New Jersey.

Printed in Great Britain
by Amazon.co.uk, Ltd.,
Marston Gate.